WINTER WISHES AT THE FARM ON MUDDYPUDDLE LANE

Heart-warming, uplifting romance

Etti Summers

CHAPTER ONE

If Mark Stafford didn't get this damned book written soon, he was toast.

Throwing his pen down in exasperation, he leant back in his chair, put his hands behind his head, and stared out of the window of his small office, blowing out his cheeks. What was the deadline again? Oh, yes, the end of February.

He checked the calendar, praying it was a leap year so he would have an extra day. God knows, the way he was going, he would need it.

The house opposite flashed into life as their many Christmas decorations all lit up at once. It wasn't properly dark yet, but the November afternoon was overcast and gloomy. Unfortunately, the Santa waving at him from an illuminated ladder hanging from one of the bedroom windows did nothing for his lack of festive cheer. In fact, it made his grumpiness worse. Thank goodness neither his agent nor his editor could see him now; they'd think he was a proper Grinch, and that simply wouldn't do since he was supposed to be writing a Christmas book.

When the idea of writing a festive story had been pitched to him, he should have come clean and confessed that Christmas wasn't his cup of eggnog. But he'd thought he could pull it off, so he'd agreed. Yet, five weeks into the project, he had nothing. No characters, no storyline and no inspiration. The situation was made even more annoying because this wasn't his first book, nor even his third. Mark had written eleven books in his career, so why was he finding this one so blimmin' difficult?

It wasn't as though he had to write a three-hundred-page novel. He was a children's author, whose target readers were four to seven years old. The book would be thirty-five to fifty pages maximum, **including** the illustrations.

Mark was the first to argue that writing children's books wasn't easy. The author had to appeal to both the child **and** the parent, and fewer words didn't mean less effort or dedication. It was different, that's all – a difference he'd thought he'd mastered.

Clearly not, if today's miserably disappointing effort was any indication.

It didn't help that the publisher wanted a title and the cover art in the next couple of weeks so they could begin the marketing process. But how could he give them that, when he had no idea what the story was going to be about?

His neighbour's manically waving Santa Claus was becoming irritating, so Mark lowered the blind. The afternoon had drawn in, and as much as he enjoyed taking a break from working by gazing into the street, he'd found himself doing considerably more gazing than working. Resting his eyes was one thing, but these past few days his peepers seemed to have taken a vacation.

He scowled, feeling hemmed in and claustrophobic. Maybe he should get some fresh air? It might clear his head.

Actually, there wasn't anything to clear. That was the problem – his head was empty. Perhaps filling it with Christmassy stuff might help? He could pay the city centre a visit and soak up some atmosphere. The festivities weren't in full swing yet, but there should be enough Christmas spirit around to get him in the mood.

Deciding this was as good a plan as any, he donned his padded jacket and plonked a knitted beanie on his head. It wasn't unduly cold out, but an annoyingly fine drizzle hung in the air.

The bus stop was a five-minute walk from his house, so rather than drive and try to grapple with Bristol's awful rush-hour traffic, he decided to hop on a bus. It would also mean he needn't worry about parking, which could be a nightmare. He would even have a bite to eat whilst he was out, because his fridge was rather empty and the freezer was equally as bad. He really should make more of an effort in the kitchen, but although he enjoyed cooking, he couldn't be bothered just for himself. Now and again he would have a frenzy and bulk cook lots of stuff, but that didn't happen regularly enough to keep his freezer stocked with home-made dishes. The only meals in there right now were of the ready variety, and none of them appealed.

His thoughts were still on food when the bus trundled into The Horsefair, and he hopped off at the next stop. The street was busy with people scurrying along the pavements, and shops were already belting out Christmas tunes, their window displays full of festive cheer. Overhead, twinkly lights were strung across the street and the lamp posts boasted flashing stars and snowflakes. Mark ducked into a store selling decorations, wandered aimlessly around it and then ducked out again, not having found what he was searching for.

He had yet to find it fifty minutes and numerous shops later, so he gave up and headed for a little place he knew on Philadelphia Street where the food was good.

As he ate, it suddenly came to him that he was trying to recapture the feeling that he used to have when he was a child. Christmas had been such a wonderful, magical time then, and the sheer excitement he'd felt had been overwhelming.

Mark stared at the pasta in the wide-rimmed bowl and shook his head. He was thirty-nine years old and hadn't been a child for a very long time, so how the hell did he think he could ever feel that way again? But his instinct – that gut feeling he always listened to when it came to his storytelling – was insistent that was what he needed to do. If he wanted to make this next book shine and sparkle, he needed to remember what it was like to be a child at Christmas.

Perhaps going on a writing retreat would help? He'd done something similar before; when he'd written the seaside series he had rented a house on the coast for three months to immerse himself in all things harbour and beach-related.

Mark realised he was looking for inspiration in the wrong place. Bristol wasn't it.

However, Picklewick, the small village where he'd grown up, might very well be.

Beatrice Webb let out yet another exasperated sigh. Getting her children ready for school was a daily battle and she didn't think she had the energy for another skirmish this week, but as today was only Thursday, she still had one more to go until the blessed weekend.

The murky mornings at this time of year didn't help, because Taya, at nine years old, was becoming a real lug-a-bed and was as grumpy as hell at being woken.

Five-year-old Sadie was the opposite —
up like a lark and raring to go.
Unfortunately, Sadie's lark had risen at
five-thirty, and by **raring to go,** Beatrice
wasn't referring to school. Sadie tried
everything to delay going, from hiding her
school shoes to having a full-blown
meltdown, and this morning she was
insisting she had to write a letter to Santa
and it had to be done before school so it
could be posted on the way.

'Taya, please go brush your teeth,'
Beatrice instructed, as she tried to wrestle
her youngest daughter's hair into
submission.

'I haven't finished my breakfast.' Taya
had been reading instead of eating.

Although Beatrice had asked her not to
read at the table, Taya had ignored her.
She'd been tempted to snatch the book

out of her daughter's hands but, for one, she didn't want to deal with the fallout, and secondly she knew how lucky she was that she didn't have to nag her child to read, the way many of her friends had to nag theirs.

'Please get a move on,' she urged. Turning to Sadie, she said, 'All done.'

Sadie patted the top of her head. 'I wanted plaits, not bunches.'

'You look lovely with bunches.'

'But I wanted plaits.'

'I haven't got time to do plaits. Sadie, get dressed. You too, Taya.'

Sadie smacked her pencil down on the table. 'I'm **not** going to school with my hair in bunches.'

Beatrice counted to five. 'When I asked you how you wanted your hair, you said you didn't know.'

'Well I do now, and I want plaits.'

She briefly considered fetching her scissors and snipping the offending bunches off. It would solve the problem – but in turn would generate a much bigger one.

'Taya, if you don't put your uniform on in the next five minutes, you'll be going to school in your pyjamas,' she warned.

Taya gave her a 'yeah, right' look and slowly got to her feet. Taking her book with her, she dawdled out of the kitchen.

With a sigh of relief that at least one of her children was doing as she was told, Beatrice turned her attention to her youngest daughter. 'Come on, it's time you got dressed too.'

Beatrice shot a look of longing at the toaster, but she knew she would be needed upstairs, despite Sadie being more than capable of dressing herself. If she wanted to get her kids to school on time, she would have to forgo breakfast. Telling herself that her waistline would thank her for it, she cleared away the breakfast things – and by **clearing away** she meant dumping them on the draining board to be dealt with later.

'Mummy, I'm going to ask Santa for a Wixset for Christmas,' Sadie announced.

Beatrice blinked. What's a Wixset, she wondered.

'And a talking puppy that wees and poops, because you won't let me have a real one. And a scooter. Not like my old scooter – I want one you plug in. It goes really fast. And I want a tiara. A proper one, not a plastic one.'

Ushering her reluctant daughter into the hall and up the stairs, Beatrice said faintly, 'I'm not sure Father Christmas can stretch to all that. It's rather a lot.'

'No, it isn't.' Sadie's reply was confident. 'Penelope had a scooter and a Wixset from her mummy for her birthday, and her granny and grandad got her a Poopy Puppy, and her dad bought her a tiara. It's got real diamonds. Penelope said so.'

Oh well, if **Penelope** said so, Beatrice grumbled silently to herself. Even without knowing what a Wixset was, she had a suspicion that that little lot would cost a fortune.

Sadie hadn't finished. 'And I want a head.'

Beatrice steered her into the bedroom and helped her remove her pyjamas. 'Just a head? No body?'

Sadie nodded. 'Just a head. I want to learn to do plaits, because the ones you do fall out.'

'Oh, right. Okay. A head with hair.' Beatrice used to have one of those when she was a girl.

'Duh! **Of course** with hair. Silly Mummy.'

The door to the bedroom bounced open as Taya stormed in. 'Mum!' she cried, 'I need a new school bag. The strap has broken.' She waved the offending item in Beatrice's face, and Beatrice's heart sank further when her daughter asked, 'Can I pick the next one?' because she simply knew it would be the one all her friends had and would be hideously expensive.

Not for the first time since her youngest had started school in September, Beatrice thought about getting a part-time job. But the problem was, finding one which fitted in around school times was as likely as the diamonds in Penelope's tiara being real.

'Mrs Webb, can I have a quick word?'

Beatrice saw Sadie's teacher beckoning her from the door of the classroom, and her heart sank for the second time that morning. A teacher **wanting a word** was never good, plus Beatrice had hoped to make a quick getaway, considering Sadie had walked into the classroom without any drama, but seeing Miss Barnes talking to her might evoke some.

Miss Barnes seemed equally as concerned, as she glanced over her shoulder. 'Nothing to worry about,' she said. 'I just wanted to inform you that Sadie is going to be Toadstool Number One in the Christmas play, and I know she wanted to be a fairy so she'll probably be a little disappointed when she finds out. But the fairies are all Year Three children as there's quite a lot of dancing, and...' She ground to a halt.

Beatrice said, 'Thanks for the heads up.' She was going to have to find some way of bigging up the toadstool role. Knowing her daughter's penchant for pink and silver, a sparkly pink number might do the trick. 'Can the toadstool be any colour?' she asked.

'Oh, yes. Just use whatever spare material you've got lying around.'

Bless her. From what Beatrice could gather, this was the teacher's first year in the classroom. She had an awful lot to learn about the competitive nature of certain mums. And although Beatrice didn't want to spend hours making a costume which would only be worn for a matter of hours, she wasn't going to let her daughter down by having her wear a substandard outfit. Maybe she could enlist some help in making it?

It was a good idea to strike while the iron was hot (in other words, before her enthusiasm waned or she forgot) so Beatrice decided to call in to see her mum on the way home. Thinking it best not to arrive empty handed, she popped into the bakery on the way and picked up a selection of cream cakes.

As she was passing the newsagents, being careful not to jostle the cake box, she automatically glanced at the window and the notices that were pinned there.

And stopped.

Frowning, she stepped closer and peered at a **Help Wanted** sign. The farm on Muddypuddle Lane was advertising for an assistant for their newly opened farm shop. Experience preferred, hours negotiable.

How negotiable? she wondered.

There was only one way to find out, but first she'd have to have a chat with her mum. There was no point in getting her hopes up if Mum didn't feel able to help out with childcare during the school holidays or at the weekends.

Her mum was delighted to see her, but that was probably more to do with the cream cake offering than with seeing Beatrice herself. Her mum mightn't be so delighted when she heard the favours Beatrice wanted to ask.

She decided to begin with the easiest first and said brightly, 'Sadie is going to be a toadstool in the Christmas play.'

Deborah was examining the cakes. 'Toadstools aren't particularly festive, are they?' She picked up a cream horn with her fingers. 'I'll leave the coffee puff for your dad.'

'You wouldn't leave it for Dad if **you** liked it,' Beatrice teased. Mum couldn't stand anything coffee flavoured, although she enjoyed a latte as much as the next person.

Deborah took a bite of her cake and said around the mouthful, 'I suppose you want some help making it?'

'You don't have to,' Beatrice assured her.

'I think I do if you don't want it to fall apart after five minutes.'

'Harsh.'

'But true,' her mum countered with a smile. 'I'll see what I can find. Put the kettle on, if you're staying.'

Beatrice couldn't leave yet, so she filled the kettle and switched it on. 'Mum, can I ask you something? Please say no, if you don't think you can. I know we've talked about it in the past, but you've had a taste of freedom and—'

'You've got a job?' Deborah beamed at her.

'Not yet. There's one going up at the farm on Muddypuddle Lane.'

'Doing what? You don't know anything about sheep or cows, and think of the dirt. Plus, you'll be out in all weathers.' Her mother shuddered.

'They want someone for the shop.'

Deborah's face cleared. 'Oh, yes. I'd forgotten about that. Phew, that's a relief. I had visions of you in overalls and wellies. Of course I'll look after the girls. I love having them.'

'I don't know the hours yet and they might want someone for the weekends,' Beatrice warned.

Her parents had retired earlier in the year and although Beatrice had discussed the possibility of going back to work with them, she didn't want them to feel obliged – after all, they deserved to enjoy their retirement, and although they adored their grandchildren, the kids weren't their responsibility.

'I'll phone the farm later and find out,' she said. 'Anyway, they mightn't want me.'

Her mum popped the last of her cake into her mouth and licked her fingers. 'How could they not want **you**, my darling girl?'

'You're biased,' Beatrice replied, but she hoped her mum was right. With Christmas approaching, she needed all the money she could get her hands on.

Picklewick was much the same as he remembered, Mark thought as he drove along the high street, heading towards the one and only pub where he would be staying for the next couple of weeks. After deciding yesterday that this was the place to be, he had wasted no time in throwing some clothes in a case this morning and setting off. After all, he didn't have anything keeping him in Bristol.

No, Picklewick hadn't changed – it was Mark himself who had.

Intrinsically, the village appeared the same as he remembered, but it felt new and strange, as though the past was a foreign land whose soil he now walked.

He hadn't been back to the area since his parents had moved to a bungalow in Bath, and that had been years ago. And even when they'd still lived in Picklewick, his visits had been fleeting, never for more than a long weekend, because his wife had found the village boring. Ex-wife, now; and the irony of her marrying a hotelier who lived in the wilds of Scotland still made him chuckle. He wondered how bored she was now.

The Black Horse came into view, and he smiled as he caught sight of the familiar sign hanging above the door. It swung in the stiff breeze, and when he got out of the car he could hear it creaking. The sound brought back memories, but he pushed them aside. He would have plenty of time to think about his misspent youth in this very establishment after he'd checked in and unpacked.

The landlord didn't recognise him at first. 'Here for work?' Dave asked as he showed him to his room.

'You could say that.'

'A couple of weeks, is it?'

'There or thereabouts.'

Dave unlocked a door. 'This is yours. Number three. You've got this floor all to yourself at the moment, so it'll be nice and quiet – apart from the noise from the bar of course, although it shouldn't be too bad as it never gets rowdy. Unless it's karaoke night, and then it can get a bit loud.' The landlord winced. 'Some of the singing leaves a lot to be desired. But Thursday is quiz night so it should be quiet enough this evening. Do you quiz?'

'Not really.'

The landlord was squinting at him, a puzzled expression on his face, then he slapped a palm to his forehead. '**Mark Stafford**! I should have realised, but it didn't twig. Long time, no see. How are you?'

'Good, thanks.'

'And your mum and dad?'

'They're living their best life in Bath.'

'I heard that's where they'd moved to. What about you? Do you live in Bath, too?'

Mark shook his head. 'Bristol.'

'Not too far from them, then. You're here for work, you say?'

Mark rarely broadcast what he did for a living, preferring to fly under the radar, but he decided to give the man a half-version of the truth.

'I'm an illustrator. Books,' he added, before Dave asked the inevitable question.

'Covers, like?'

'Sometimes.'

'Right. And you'll be working here?'

Mark guessed what the man was thinking. 'Don't worry, I won't splash paint everywhere. I'm a digital artist.'

'That's a relief. The missus would throw a fit if you got paint on her carpet.' He handed Mark an old-fashioned key. 'Breakfast between eight and nine?

'Perfect.'

'Any special requirements?'

'None whatsoever.'

'Right, I'll leave you to it. If you need anything, just shout. We serve food in the bar from noon until nine p.m.'

'Thanks. I'll be down soon for a spot of lunch.'

Dave took his leave, but not before pointing to a slim folder on the dressing table. 'Local information,' he said, adding, 'Not that you'll need it.'

As Mark unpacked, he didn't think he would need it either, but when he gave its contents a cursory once-over, he was mildly surprised to be proved wrong. There was some kind of an event – a Christmas Wonderland – at the farm on Muddypuddle Lane on Saturday, and he intended to take a look.

'Pop up now, if you like.' That was what Dulcie Fairfax, the owner of the farm on Muddypuddle Lane had said when Beatrice rang to enquire about the job after she'd left her mum's house.

Concerned because she didn't have a CV prepared, and neither did she have anything smart enough to wear for an interview, Beatrice felt nervous and out of her depth as she drove into the farmyard later that morning.

She had managed to find a pair of black tailored trousers at the back of her wardrobe which hadn't seen the light of day for several years, and she teamed it with a cream blouse that gaped a bit around the boobs because she'd put on weight since having Sadie. So rather than look as though she was bursting out of it, she wore a black vest top underneath and left the buttons undone. Her black ankle boots were tidy enough, and when she stepped out of her car she was glad she'd worn them and not the high heels that she'd bought to go to a friend's wedding, as the farmyard was cobbled and uneven.

Beatrice looked around with interest. A huge tree sat in the centre of the yard, decorated but unlit; there was a kiosk with a chalkboard sign on it advertising The Grinch's Grotto, pony rides and various other activities; and there were several barn-type buildings, as well as the farmhouse.

A woman wearing scruffy jeans, wellies and an oversized hoodie emerged from one of the buildings, and Beatrice recognised her as the woman who'd won the farm in a raffle. The farm had originally belonged to Walter York and had been in his family for generations, but rumour was that he'd been in financial difficulties, with the result that the farm had been raffled off. Beatrice had bought a ticket, but it was Dulcie – a complete newbie when it came to farming – who had won it. She seemed to be coping alright now though.

'Beatrice? I'm Dulcie.' The woman hurried forward, holding out a hand.

Beatrice shook it nervously, suddenly feeling overdressed. She knew **of** her (how could she not, with Picklewick being so small?) but they'd never actually met, and she wasn't sure what to expect.

Dulcie said, 'Come through into the kitchen. I don't know about you, but I'm gasping for a cuppa.' She strode towards the farmhouse and Beatrice followed, picking her way carefully over the muddy cobbles.

'Tea or coffee?' she asked, after inviting Beatrice to take a seat at the chunky oak table in the kitchen.

'Nothing, thanks,' Beatrice replied, gazing around her in awe. This wasn't how she expected a farmhouse kitchen to look –

this was something out of a cookery show on TV.

Dulcie noticed her interest. 'This is Otto's domain, not mine. He owns The Wild Side in the village.'

Beatrice knew who he was. **Everyone** in Picklewick knew that Otto York had been a renowned London chef. She also knew that he'd grown up in Picklewick and used to live on this very farm. But that was as far as it went – he had been a couple of years below her in school, so she hadn't had anything to do with him, and then he'd moved away and had made a name for himself. Like someone else she could mention, she thought, then gave herself a silent telling off – she was in the middle of a job interview, for Pete's sake! Now wasn't the time to be reminiscing about old boyfriends.

'It's nice,' she said, dragging her attention back to the present, her eyes roaming over the stainless-steel units.

'We've only just had it installed. You should have seen it before! Anyway, are you sure you don't want a drink? I'm having one, and I'm also going to have a red velvet crackle cookie. Otto's been experimenting with a festive version.'

'Okay then, thanks. Tea, please.'

Dulcie was really down to earth and as Beatrice sipped her tea and nibbled on her cookie (which really was rather moreish), Dulcie filled her in about the shop, which was also new, having only opened a couple of weeks ago.

'I can't manage everything by myself,' she explained. 'The business is really taking off, and I'm struggling. If you've finished your tea, let me show you around. We'll start with the shop first, since that's where you'll be working.' She led Beatrice outside and they walked back across the yard, towards one of the outbuildings. 'We sell fresh produce such as goat's milk, cheese, eggs and any fruit and veg that are in season and we've got a surplus of, so that can vary from week to week – day to day, even.' She came to a halt outside a door and pushed it open.

Beatrice scanned the room – a chiller, a counter, shelves... Everything looked clean and tidy. Festive bunting was draped around the walls and fairy lights twinkled behind the counter.

Dulcie said, 'We milk the goats every day, although the yield isn't great at this time of year and neither is egg production, but we're hoping the Christmas bits and pieces will make up for it. We've got handmade soap, lotions and potions, biscuits, pastries, savouries, milkshakes, soups... And we're hoping for a good turnout tomorrow for the first of our Christmas Wonderland events, and we've got lots of things planned. You might have noticed a sign for the Grinch's Grotto?'

Beatrice nodded, her eyes everywhere, and she felt a spark of excitement. She could really see herself working here.

'Come on, I'll show you the rest of it.'

The rest consisted of a barn with goats, a sheep, chickens (who were roaming free), a couple of Shetland ponies (borrowed from the stables down the lane), and rabbits. A fantastic grotto which was very in keeping with the Grinch's story, was in another building, along with a creative area where kids could make Christmas crafts, and a kitchen.

Dulcie said. 'We'll be selling mulled wine, soup, coffees, hot chocolate and anything else Otto dreams up.'

'You said the hours are negotiable?' Beatrice asked hesitantly, guessing they wouldn't be as negotiable as she would need them to be.

'What hours can you do?' Dulcie asked, and when Beatrice told her, she said, 'I'm sure we can work around that. When can you start?'

'Whenever you want.'

'How about tomorrow?'

'But you don't know anything about me!' Beatrice protested. Dulcie hadn't asked how she would deal with an awkward customer, or about her strengths and weaknesses, or any of the other questions she had anxiously expected.

'Walter, Otto's dad, does. He knows your father and he vouched for you. Besides, it's more important to me that we get on. I don't care about retail experience. What I care about is personality.' Dulcie beamed at her. 'So, **can** you start tomorrow?'

'Absolutely!'

'Fab. See you in the morning. By the way, you might want to dress down a bit.'

Beatrice glanced at her blouse and trousers, caught Dulcie's eye, and the two of them burst out laughing. She was going to like working here!

'Mummy has got some news,' Beatrice said to Sadie later that evening as she pulled back the covers for her daughter to dive into bed. She had already told Taya, who hadn't expressed much interest.

'Story,' Sadie demanded.

'Don't you want to hear my news?' Beatrice pretended to pout.

Sadie sat up and folded her arms. 'What is it?' she sighed, rolling her eyes.

Beatrice saw herself in the gesture. 'I've got a job, so Nanny will fetch you from school tomorrow, okay?' Although her official hours were ten until three and she should be finished in time to collect the children, she didn't want to have to worry on her first day.

Sadie's expression didn't change.

'I'm going to be working in a shop,' Beatrice continued.

'A toy shop?' Sadie's eyes lit up.

'Not a toy shop. It's a—'

'Sweet shop!' She wriggled excitedly.

'No, not a sweet shop, either.'

Her daughter's face fell.

'It's a farm shop,' Beatrice said, then hastily added, 'Selling milk, cheese and fruit. Stuff like that,' in case Sadie thought she would be selling actual farms.

'Do they have animals?'

'They certainly do! Goats, chickens and rabbits. Dulcie, who owns the farm, said they have a cat, but I didn't see it.'

'Can I see the rabbits?'

'Yes, and you can see the goats, too.'

'Tomorrow?'

'Not tomorrow, but soon.' Dulcie had explained that the farm was organising activities on the run-up to Christmas and opening its doors to the public and when Beatrice heard what Dulcie was planning, she knew her daughters would love it.

'Enough questions,' Beatrice said. 'It's time for a story. What would you like?'

'That one!' Sadie pointed to a book on the top of the small pile on her bedside table.

'Not again,' Beatrice groaned.

'Yes again.'

'Okay, budge over.'

Sadie scooted across the bed and smuggled under the bedclothes, so her mum could sit next to her.

Beatrice reached for the book, and as she did so the author's name caught her eye and she winced.

It had been written by Mark Stafford – the man who had broken her heart.

CHAPTER TWO

Friday was one of those bright winter days where a weak sun shone out of a silvered sky and mist blanketed the valley floor. Dew-coated cobwebs were spider-strung over the bushes along Muddypuddle Lane, and the red berries of the hawthorn trees glistened like rubies in the morning light.

Beatrice parked her car in the farmyard and took a deep breath of autumn-chilled air. This was her first day in her new job and she couldn't imagine a more scenic location. At the moment, she felt incredibly blessed; whether she would still feel that way after a five-hour shift remained to be seen.

The tree in the centre of the yard was lit and it looked very festive, despite Christmas being five weeks away. But, as Dulcie had explained when Beatrice had come for the interview (which hadn't been much of an interview at all), the farm was gearing up to open its gates to visitors who would hopefully enjoy the Christmas experience.

Beatrice was rather looking forward to it and had happily agreed to work Saturdays on the run-up to the 'Big Day' because it meant more money to buy presents. However, she wasn't doing this **just** for the money. Beatrice was also doing it for herself. The pride she'd felt knowing she had a job, had made her glow all last night, and as soon as the children were tucked up in bed, she'd got straight on the phone to Lisa.

Lisa had been thrilled for her, and suggested they go out for a drink to celebrate but Beatrice had declined – she was already putting her mum out by asking her to collect the children from school. She could hardly ask her to babysit this evening as well, while she went out boozing with her best friend.

Dulcie was serving a customer when Beatrice entered the shop, so she quietly stowed her bag and coat underneath the counter and had a quick look at the chillers and shelves to see what was for sale today.

The farm's staples of milk, cheese, eggs, soaps and scented candles were well stocked, and she was also pleased to see a selection of festive-themed biscuits, milkshakes and chilled soups.

Dulcie greeted her warmly, looking frazzled. 'Am I glad to see you! I've got such a lot to do today. I've got a Grinch's grotto to finish, a seating area to set up, a—' She stopped. 'I could go on, but if I do I'll be jabbering away until lunchtime. Will you be alright in here on your own?'

'I'll be fine.'

'Shout if you need me. Oh, and do you think you could have a go at making up some festive hampers? I want to post photos on the website later.' Dulcie pointed to a box behind the counter. 'Here's one I made earlier,' she said. 'I'd like to offer different products and a couple of different sizes.'

'Is there anything else I can do to help?' Beatrice offered.

'You might regret saying that.' Dulcie pulled a face. 'I'd better get going. I've got smelly socks to fill. Actually, you don't happen to have any odd socks lying around at home, do you?'

Beatrice chuckled. Knowing that the farm had a Grinch theme going on, she realised immediately why Dulcie wanted them. 'I've got a drawer full. I'll bring them in tomorrow. How many do you need?'

'All of them? I'm scared we won't have enough, but I'm also worried that I've ordered too much, and we'll have loads of stuff left over.'

'What are you putting in them?'

'Grinch dust – you sprinkle it on your doorstep to stop the Grinch stealing your Christmas – bags of green sweets, a Grinch bauble for the tree, Grinch Stickers and a stretchy Grinch toy.'

'I sense a theme,' Beatrice laughed. 'It's also rather a lot, don't you think?'

'Is it?' Dulcie's expression was dubious.

'It must have cost a bit, and whenever my two visited Santa in his grotto, the gift was usually something inexpensive. How many children are you expecting? By the way, is it alright if my parents bring the girls to see the Grinch tomorrow?'

'Of course it is! As for how many kids – I honestly don't know.'

Beatrice had an idea, but she hadn't been here five minutes yet, so she wasn't sure how well it would be received. 'I've got a suggestion – and please tell me if I'm speaking out of turn because you know more about this than I do.'

'Don't bet on it,' Dulcie said.

'Why don't you keep some stuff back, and add a Grinch biscuit to the sock instead?' She looked at the iced snowflake biscuits as she spoke, thinking it would be easy to make a green version.

Dulcie was staring at her and shaking her head.

Oh dear, Beatrice thought, that didn't go down well.

'I could kiss you!' her new boss declared with a smile.

'You could?'

'That's a perfect solution. Otto can make an endless supply of Grinch cookies, and if we do have any non-food items left over, they'll keep until next year. The Grinch isn't going away – I'm determined to get my use out of the outfits I bought, and the grotto.'

Beatrice offered, 'If you want, I can fill the socks for you tomorrow.'

From the grateful expression on Dulcie's face, she **did** want.

Pleased that she'd already managed to make herself useful, Beatrice settled down to enjoy the day. She had a feeling that this job was going to be the best thing to have happened to her in a very long time.

For Mark, driving up Muddypuddle Lane on Saturday afternoon brought back boyhood memories of warm summer days playing in the ferns on the hillsides above Picklewick with his friends, making dens and building makeshift dams across the tumbling mountain streams.

It also brought back memories of when he was quite a bit older and had gone on long walks on this very hillside with his first love.

He wondered whether she still lived in Picklewick. The last he'd heard was that she was married with a baby, but that was ages ago.

Mark drove past the stables and continued up the lane until he came to the farm. A sign directed him to the rear of a large barn where there was a gravelled parking area. It was surprisingly busy for a dreary Saturday afternoon in November, and he felt a glimmer of hope that maybe the farm would kickstart his flagging creativity.

The place certainly looked festive. Fairy lights and lanterns were strung everywhere, a twenty-foot tree sat in the middle of the yard, and next to the entrance to the barn was a red post box with a sign above it urging children to "post your letter to Santa here".

Mark paused for a moment to admire the tree. Someone had gone to a lot of trouble to decorate it. But although it was very pretty, it failed to move the dial on his internal festive-ometer.

Glancing around, he saw signs for a shop, a Christmas kitchen, a craft barn and a Grinch's Grotto, and excited chatter and squealing filled the air as children queued with their parents.

Feeling self-conscious because he didn't have a small person with him, he thought it best to have a word with whoever was running the place, to let them know why he was here.

As he debated whether to wait in line to explain to the elderly lady selling the tickets or whether to go into the shop and ask, his attention was caught by a woman dancing across the yard. She was dressed as an elf and was beaming so widely that he couldn't help smiling as he made to intercept her.

'Excuse me?' he said.

'Don't you just love Christmas?' she smiled, coming to a stop.

'Not as much as some,' he replied, raising an eyebrow at her outfit. 'Can you point me in the direction of the manager or the owner?'

Her smile dimmed. 'May I ask why?'

'Don't worry, it's not a complaint or anything. I just need to have a word.'

'Are you from Environmental Health?' The smile had entirely gone.

'Not at all.'

She pursed her lips then nodded. 'Come into the house. Will this take long?'

'A couple of minutes, tops.'

'Good, because the Grinch needs a comfort break. He'll get grouchy if he has to cross his legs.'

Bemused, Mark followed her into the house, then blinked when she led him into a state-of-the-art kitchen. 'Wow.'

'Yeah, I know. I'm too scared to use it. My partner, Otto, had it installed. He owns The Wild Side in the village.'

'Ah, yes, the restaurant.' Mark hadn't eaten there yet, having taken his evening meals in The Black Horse, but he intended to give it a go at some point.

The woman leant against one of the stainless-steel units and folded her arms. 'I'm Dulcie Fairfax and this is my farm. What do you want to have a word with me about?'

'My name is Mark Stafford and I'm a children's author. I was born and bred in Picklewick, although I live in Bristol now, and I've come to the village to write my next book. Or to get ideas for it, at the very least.'

'What's that got to do with my farm?'

'I'm a bit low on festive spirit and it's a Christmas story, so I'm hoping your Christmas Wonderland might help.'

Dulcie's stern expression softened. 'A real-life Grinch, eh?'

He dredged up a smile. 'You could say that.'

'So, why did you need to speak with me?'

'Because I want to pay a visit to The Grinch's Grotto and as I haven't brought a child with me, I thought it might look a bit weird.'

'You're right, it may have done. Would you like me to see if I can find one for you to borrow?'

Mark was aghast. 'No, I—'

'Just joking,' she laughed. 'Go ahead and look all you want. Would you like me to show you around?'

'That's kind of you, if you can spare the time.' He would have felt very odd going in on his own.

'I was on my way to the Grotto anyway, so it's no bother.'

She led him back across the yard, and when they reached the entrance to the Grinch's Grotto where another elf was checking children and their parents in, Dulcie said in a low voice, 'Carla, can you put the rope across for five minutes?

Walter needs a break.' Then she ushered him inside.

Mark hadn't known what to expect when he stepped into the barn, so he was pleasantly surprised to see it as exuberantly decorated as the yard. More lights, more bunting, and more lavishly decorated trees surrounded by mounds of fake snow, formed a path which led deeper into the barn. It was quite magical, despite being over-the-top, but as they ventured further in and turned a corner, the lights became less twinkly, the bunting disappeared, and the trees lost their decorations.

It was a gradual thing, and Mark didn't notice at first, not until a structure that had been painted to look like a cave came into view. A **Santa Stop Here** sign was in front of the door, and someone had written **'Don't'** between **Santa** and **Stop**.

Three families were waiting to see the Grinch and as Mark and his guide approached, the door opened and a green face topped by a Santa hat, peered out.

'Bah! I hate Christmas!' it growled, then disappeared back inside and slammed the door shut. A second later, the door opened again, and the Grinch beckoned the nearest child forward. Mark caught a glimpse of a badly decorated and extremely bent Christmas tree, and a haphazard pile of presents stacked in the corner. Lying by the door and gnawing on a bone, was a black and white sheepdog wearing felt antlers.

The theme was green, red and white, and rather well done, but Mark's festive-ometer still didn't budge. The Grinch had originally been drawn in black, white and red. It wasn't supposed to be green, and **this** was why he was having so much trouble writing a Christmas book – because he couldn't get his head around the way everything about Christmas was so distorted. Take St. Nicolas, for instance...

Dulcie waited until the Grinch had seen all three children and the families had left the grotto, then said, 'Break time, Walter?'

The Grinch sagged a little. 'Thank God.' He pulled off the mask and took a deep breath, and Mark saw that underneath it was an elderly gentleman with grey hair and a lined face. He looked exhausted.

Dulcie helped him out of the costume. 'Are you okay to carry on, Walter, or would you like me to take over?'

'You have enough to do,' he said. 'How long have I got?'

'Ten minutes, but we can make it longer.'

He blew out his cheeks. 'Do you mind?'

'Of course not. I'll let Carla know.' She hurried towards the entrance, leaving Mark alone with Walter.

The elderly gent said, 'This is the first time she's done this. Just a couple of teething troubles, that's all. I'm sure everything will work out fine.'

Mark wasn't so sure; Walter didn't look too good and as Mark watched him leave, he wondered whether he should say anything to Dulcie or whether he should mind his own business.

But when Dulcie returned to the grotto, he could tell by her face that she already knew.

She picked up the discarded costume and sighed. 'I don't think it's a good idea for Walter to carry on. It's too much for him. Right, I'd better do it. Have you seen enough, or do you need more time to find your Christmas spirit?' Dulcie froze, her eyes widening. Then a smile spread across her face as she stared at him.

Mark guessed what was coming, and he shook his head as he backed away. 'Nuh-uh. Not a chance.'

'Aw, go on,' she pleaded. 'Just think of all those hopeful little faces – and you can indulge your inner Grinch at the same time. I'll even pay you,' she added, and he realised she was serious.

'You'd trust me with this?' He waved an arm at the grotto.

'Yes.'

'You don't even know me.'

Dulcie fished around in the pocket of the pixie skirt and brought out a phone. 'I looked you up.'

'When?'

'Just now. You've made appearances in schools and libraries. You **like** kids.'

'I do, but I don't like Christmas. Anyway, I'm here to write,' he protested.

'Research is writing.'

'Who says?'

'You do.' She showed him the screen.

Mark groaned. On it was an interview where he had given advice to new authors. He remembered stressing how important research was when it came to writing.

'Just for today?' she pleaded. 'Three hours, at the most. Please?'

And that was how Mark Stafford, successful children's author, came to be dressed in a Grinch costume, trying his best to entertain small children on the farm on Muddypuddle Lane.

Beatrice was so busy she didn't know what to do with herself and was loving every minute of it. The hampers were flying off the shelves, as were the gift boxes of soaps, and every time the door opened she caught a whiff of mulled wine along with a blast of cold air, which made her thankful for her many layers and for the electric heater behind the counter that kept her legs and feet warm.

Things appeared to be going equally as well outside the shop. Although Beatrice didn't have a view of the barn, from the snippets she'd overheard from her customers, there was a queue to see the Grinch, the petting area was popular, and the food was going down a storm. In order to encourage repeat custom over the next few weeks, Dulcie and Otto were varying the food on the menu, hoping to tempt visitors back, and there was also a selection of today's offerings in the shop, so if people wanted they could purchase some to take home.

Beatrice didn't know how Dulcie and Otto managed to fit it all in, although they had some help in the form of Dulcie's mum Beth, and Otto's dad Walter, plus Nikki, one of Dulcie's sisters, and a couple of others. But it was still a lot of work, and whenever she glanced out the window she saw Dulcie dashing around in her pixie outfit.

Between serving customers, Beatrice filled the 'smelly socks,' and made up more hampers, and as she worked she kept an eye on the time.

Her parents were due to arrive shortly with the children, and she couldn't wait to see her girls' faces. Sadie had been so excited this morning at the prospect of meeting the Grinch, that she hadn't stopped talking. Mind you, she was also thrilled at the thought of stroking a goat, petting a rabbit and having a ride on a Shetland pony. Taya hadn't been quite as enthusiastic, but she was nearly ten, which was almost a grown-up as far as Taya was concerned, and such childish things were beneath her.

Beatrice was gift-wrapping a box of soaps when she noticed her dad peering through the window, waving to catch her attention.

'Two minutes?' she mouthed, and as soon as she'd served her customer, she sent a quick message to Dulcie to alert her.

Dulcie, bless her, arrived in seconds.

'I won't be long.' Beatrice assured her.

'Take as long as you need. You're due a break.'

Beatrice removed her apron. 'It looks busy out there.'

'It is!' Dulcie beamed. 'The Grinch is a big hit, and Otto can't keep up with the mince pies.'

'I've made up more socks,' Beatrice told her. 'Do you want me to take them to the grotto?'

'It's okay, I'll take them later,' Dulcie said. 'You'd better go, I think someone is getting impatient.'

Beatrice saw Sadie jumping up and down outside, tugging on her nana's hand.

'Mummy!' she cried, letting go of Deborah and barrelling towards Beatrice as soon as she stepped outside.

Sadie grabbed her around the waist and buried her face in Beatrice's stomach.

Beatrice hugged her back. She would have liked to cuddle her eldest child too, but knew that Taya would hate it. Cuddles in public had become a no-no recently.

As the five of them headed towards the Grinch's Grotto, Beatrice took the opportunity to look around the yard. Several families were queuing at the kiosk for tickets, and more were waiting to enter the grotto itself. There was a steady trickle of people in and out of the petting area, and the tables in the makeshift cafe were all occupied.

No wonder Dulcie was pleased. This first Saturday was proving to be a runaway success, and Beatrice was thrilled for her.

Before long, Deborah was handing their tickets to the elf on the door and they went inside. Although Dulcie had shown

Beatrice the entrance to the Grinch's Grotto when she'd come for the interview, none of the Christmas lights had been lit, and she gasped at how pretty it now looked.

Beatrice wasn't the only one who was impressed. Sadie was gazing around in awe, her cheeks glowing, her mouth open. Even Taya's eyes were wide, and Beatrice smiled: her little girl was still there, hidden beneath the urge to grow up as fast as she could.

They shuffled forward slowly, and Beatrice used the time to remind her daughters of the story of **The Grinch Who Stole Christmas**, even though it was a tradition that they watched the film every year, so they knew it inside out.

After ten minutes or so, the family in front of them were summoned into the cave by a cross face and a claw-like hand, and Beatrice's children were next in line.

'Mummy, look!' Sadie pointed to a black and white sheepdog lying next to the entrance to the Grinch's cave. It was happily gnawing on a chew, and there was a bowl of water beside it. But what made Beatrice smile were the felt antlers it wore, not on its head, but attached to a harness around its chest.

Sadie frowned. 'That isn't Max. Max is brown.' She was quite indignant.

Beatrice thought fast. The Grinch's dog **was** brown in the film. 'That's because this isn't Max. This dog's name is Rex, and he's keeping the Grinch company because Max is off practicing to be a reindeer, because he's not very good at it, is he?'

Sadie thought about it, then nodded, the explanation accepted.

Finally, it was Taya and Sadie's turn.

Beatrice watched the entrance to the cave expectantly and chuckled when the Grinch stuck his head out. He glanced at them, paused, then went back inside as though he couldn't stand the sight of them, and slammed the door shut.

The girls looked up at her. 'Is he coming back out?' Sadie asked.

'We'll have to wait and see,' Beatrice said.

A few seconds later, he shouted, 'What are you waiting for? Come in if you must.'

'Ooh, he's really grumpy, isn't he?' Beatrice said to the children, as she ushered them inside, then she said to her mum who was behind her, 'I don't think he's acting either. I reckon it's genuine.'

'Shh!' her mum hissed. 'He'll hear you.'

Beatrice giggled. 'Oops, for a minute I forgot I was working here.' Whoever the Grinch was, she didn't want to upset him, not if they had to work together. She didn't think she'd met him yet, although there was something about his voice that was familiar...

Abruptly her good mood dimmed. How bizarre that someone wearing a Grinch outfit reminded her of a man she had tried so hard to forget. And for the remainder of the brief visit to the Grinch's grotto, Beatrice kept her attention firmly on her girls.

The last person she wanted to think about right now was Mark Stafford.

'Don't bother telling me your names,' Mark said to the two children standing before him. 'I don't care. And I'm not interested in what you want for Christmas, either.' He scowled. 'Christmas shouldn't be allowed. How old are you anyway?' He aimed this comment at the younger one.

'Five.' She gazed at him confidently, not the least bit intimidated by his (or should he say *the Grinch's*) grumpiness.

'Pah! That's too old for Christmas. Or too young.'

'Why is your face green?'

'Why is yours **not green**?'

The child giggled. 'You're funny.'

'No, I'm not. I don't like funny. If I give you a smelly sock, will you go away and leave me alone?'

She nodded and he made a show of shoving a sock at them both. The eldest, a girl of about nine or ten he guessed, looked far less impressed with his performance than her sister.

The youngest one said, 'Mummy, can I give him a hug?'

'No!' he cried, louder than he meant to. 'I hate hugs, and I hate children who want to give them.' He didn't look at the mother. He daren't. But he did notice her left hand. It was ringless. Did that mean she was no longer married?

His stomach fluttered for a second, before he told himself that it didn't matter.

Mark kept the scowl on his face until Beatrice and her family left the cave, then he slumped into his seat.

He'd recognised her instantly of course. How could he not?

His whole body tingled from the shock of seeing her, and it had taken all the strength he possessed not to react. She hadn't recognised him, and he was grateful for that. How embarrassing if her first sight of him in almost twenty years was when he was dressed from head to foot in lurid green fur and wearing a rubber mask.

She hadn't changed much – she still had the same eyes. Eyes that had once looked deep into his soul. Eyes he had run away from because he had begun to fall in love with her and she hadn't loved him back.

If he'd thought for one instant that seeing her again would make him react like this, he would never have returned to Picklewick.

It briefly occurred to him that he should leave, go back to Bristol. But being in the city hadn't worked out too well for him recently, and he was here now, so... Anyway, he had only reacted like that because he hadn't expected to see her here, that was all. It had been a bit of a surprise, but he was over it now. If he bumped into her again (which he probably would, considering Picklewick wasn't very big) he'd be more prepared. Not that he had anything to prepare for. They'd dated for a while, but it hadn't been serious. She was an old flame, nothing more. Or so he told himself.

Mark drew in a deep, calming breath, then let it out in a whoosh when he heard her voice coming from just outside the grotto.

She was saying, 'I'd better get back to work. Poor Dulcie is run off her feet, and she's got more important things to do than cover for me. Stop by the shop later? I'll treat you to some snowflake biscuits to take home.'

'We will,' Beatrice's mother said. 'But don't work too hard and make sure you take a proper break.'

Mark closed his eyes and counted to ten. Beatrice worked at **the farm?**

Oh, hell. All he hoped was that he could escape with his dignity intact.

'How did the rest of your day go?' Deborah asked when Beatrice walked into her mum's house later that evening to collect the children. 'They've had their tea,' she added.

Beatrice gave her a grateful hug, then stuck her head around the living room door and told the kids to collect their things, before she answered. 'I've been rushed off my feet. The time has flown by.'

She'd loved every minute of it, thoroughly enjoying the interaction with the customers, and she'd had so much fun bringing their attention to things they hadn't considered buying, such as a Christmas Eve Box or a gingerbread milkshake. She felt part of the team already, and she really wanted Dulcie to do well.

'Thank you for bringing the girls to see the Grinch,' she added.

Once again, her thoughts turned to the man in the green costume. She had been thinking about him on and off for the rest of the afternoon and hadn't been able to shake the feeling that he reminded her of someone. His voice had been achingly familiar, but it couldn't have been...

'It was a pleasure. We loved it, and you know your father – he's a big kid himself, so he was in his element.'

'I really do appreciate you looking after them.'

'I know, sweetheart. I'm just pleased you're doing something for yourself at last.'

Beatrice gave her an arch look. 'I'm doing this for the extra money,' she replied.

'That, too,' her mum agreed. 'But I can see how much you're enjoying it. You've got some of your sparkle back.'

'Just some?' Beatrice joked weakly. She was well aware that she'd lost her sparkle. It had disappeared around the time she'd discovered that Eric had been having an affair. Then he'd disappeared too, leaving her to bring up the children on her own. Mind you, even before he'd left, Eric hadn't been much of a husband or father. At least he was an **ex**-husband now, so that was something to be grateful for.

Her mum said, 'You've not had a full sparkle for years.'

'A full sparkle? Have you been on the gin?'

'Not yet. I'm serious, Bea, you haven't.'

'These past few years have been hard.'

'You lost it before you and Eric split up.'

Beatrice shrugged. 'Two small children can rub the sparkle off anyone,' she replied. However, she knew what her mother meant. Beatrice's sparkle had begun to dim after she'd had her heart broken at the tender age of twenty-one.

It had taken her a long time to learn to love again – and look how that had turned out. Beatrice would happily do without any sparkle if it meant not being hurt again.

But it was nice that her mum thought she'd regained some, even if it was merely a glimmer and not a full-on shine.

Anyway, what was all this talk about sparkles? She needed to take the kids home and sort them out, not prattle on about sparkles.

They were taking their time, so she went into the hall and shouted for them to hurry up, and when she strolled back to the kitchen, her mum was mashing a teabag against the side of a mug with a spoon.

'I've got some gossip,' Deborah announced. 'You remember that boy you used to go out with, Mark Stafford?

Apparently, he's back. Staying at The Black Horse for a couple of weeks, so Monica says. I saw her this morning when I nipped out to fetch your dad's paper and a pint of milk. She was going into the butchers for a packet of their nice sausages, the ones with caramelised onions in them.'

Beatrice couldn't care less about the damned sausages, not when her heart was pounding and her legs felt weak at the mention of Mark's name. 'Why?' she managed. Monica ran the pub with her husband Dave, so it must be true.

Her mum looked bewildered for a moment. 'I expect there's sausage and mash on the menu today.'

'Mum, I don't care about the sausages. Why is Mark Stafford in Picklewick?'

'Work, Monica said. He's some kind of artist. She and Dave seem to think it's something to do with books, but she also said Dave might have got that wrong.'

Her mother's words washed over her, barely registering. Beatrice was too shocked to listen, because she knew **exactly** who had been hiding under that mask.

CHAPTER THREE

It was Sunday morning and Otto looked

Beatrice climbed the stairs, a pile of ironing in her arms, and tried to ignore the squabbling coming from the living room. The girls could only entertain themselves for so long, and she sensed they'd reached their limit.

The chores had to be done though, and this morning she'd managed an impressive array of cleaning, tidying, washing and ironing. In fact, she'd got carried away and had done more than she'd intended. Whenever she thought she'd finished, she managed to find something else that needed doing. The house hadn't been this clean since she'd been forced to blitz it after hosting Sadie's fifth birthday party in the summer and sixteen children had rampaged through the place.

As she entered her youngest daughter's bedroom, her eye fell on Sadie's favourite story and her lips tightened. Its author was the reason she had been unable to keep still for more than five minutes today.

Placing the ironing on the bed, she picked up the book and scowled. Beatrice had to admit that Mark told a good yarn, one that appealed to kids and adults alike, and the illustrations were gorgeous. Taya had been given it a few years ago, and if Beatrice had realised who'd written it at the time, she might well have hidden it.

Or thrown it away. But when she'd seen the name 'Mark Stafford' on the cover, she hadn't initially realised that the man she had entrusted with her heart and the children's author were one and the same. When she'd found out, she had been... not upset, exactly, but it had brought an unwelcome rush of buried feelings to the surface.

The book had become a firm favourite of Taya's and had eventually been passed on to Sadie, who loved it equally as much. Beatrice must have read the blasted thing at least a hundred times, and she was heartily sick of it – and not just of the story itself. The book was a constant reminder of a part of her life she would prefer to forget. Unfortunately for her (not for the author) the book was extremely popular so there was no escaping it. Then the damn man had gone on to publish several more. So she now pretended that the books gracing her daughter's shelf had been written by some other Mark Stafford, a Mark Stafford who she had never met and had never loved. A Mark Stafford who hadn't chosen a career instead of her. And she had succeeded up to a point, her memories safely buried underneath those that had come after – marriage, babies, divorce. **Life**.

Then yesterday happened. Why the hell had he come back? His parents had moved away years ago, so what reason could he possibly have to return to a backwater (his words) like Picklewick. "Something to do with his books" didn't sound at all believable.

And how had he ended up playing the Grinch at the farm? She was positive it had been him. Or was she?

Beatrice reached for her phone.

'Who was under the Grinch mask?' she asked Dulcie after the pleasantries were out of the way. 'I didn't think it was Walter.'

'It was originally, but this guy showed up, a children's author. He asked if he could take a look around because he's doing some research for a new book, and when we got to the grotto Walter wasn't feeling too good, so he stepped in.'

'What was his name?'

'Mark Stafford.'

'I knew it!' Beatrice muttered.

'Nikki has heard of him – his books are very popular, apparently – but I had to Google him. He was alright, wasn't he?' Dulcie sounded anxious.

'He was a brilliant Grinch,' Beatrice assured her. 'Very believable.'

'Thank goodness for that. You had me worried for a minute. He seemed really down to earth. I wanted to pay him, but he refused to take any money. That was nice of him, wasn't it?'

'It was.' Mark **was** a nice guy. Or he had been until he'd dumped her.

Her heart was thumping by the time she came off the phone, as something occurred to her. Something it shouldn't have taken this long to realise.

If **she** had recognised **him**, even with a green latex mask hiding his face, then **he** would have undoubtedly recognised **her**. And he hadn't said a word.

It wasn't working. This was Mark's third day in Picklewick and so far he had nothing, and his visit to the farm on Muddypuddle Lane on Saturday had produced zero results, despite the impromptu Grinch performance.

He still had trouble believing he'd actually agreed to it. With her powers of persuasion Dulcie would go far, he thought wryly. She'd failed to manage to talk him into a repeat performance next Saturday though. He hadn't minded helping out in an emergency, but he wasn't going to make a habit of it, especially since Beatrice worked at the farm.

It was no secret that he was back, so she was bound to get to hear of it, and there was also a possibility he might bump into her again, but he didn't want to be wearing a lurid green mask when he did.

He should go back to Bristol. It would be the sensible thing to do. If he was going to continue to suffer from writer's block, he may as well suffer from it in the comfort of his own home. He'd spent all of yesterday cooped up in this room, wracking his brains for ideas, without success, only emerging at mealtimes.

For Mark, his imagination was often sparked by an image or a scene; he would feel the urge to draw it, and from that a story would form. But nothing he'd seen in Picklewick so far had inspired him. And having Beatrice's face pop into his mind every ten seconds didn't help. She hadn't changed, she was as lovely as he remembered.

A thought drifted across his mind – what would have happened if he'd stayed in Picklewick? Might he and Beatrice have got married and had kids? A pang went through him, and he brushed it aside.

'What can I get you?' Dave asked when Mark ventured downstairs in search of a spot of lunch.

He wasn't hungry (the full English had been, well…. **full**) but he could do with a break. Staring into the distance with a blank sheet of paper in front of him, was rather demoralising.

'An Americano and a cheese and pickle sandwich, please.'

The landlord said, 'Coming right up,' but made no move to ensure that happened. Instead, he lingered, wiping a cloth across the already clean table. 'Someone called earlier, enquiring about you. A woman.'

Mark's pulse quickened. 'Who?'

'Nikki Warring. She teaches in Picklewick Primary.'

His disappointment was acute. 'What did she want?'

'She didn't say.' Dave fished a crumpled note out of his pocket. 'I was going to push this under your door, but since you're here...' He placed it on the table and Mark glanced at it.

Just a name and a mobile number, but he could guess what it was about. He'd visited many schools, nurseries and libraries since his first book was published.

The landlord hadn't moved, clearly hoping Mark would phone Nikki Warring at this very moment.

'Sandwich?' Mark reminded him.

'Yes. Right.' With a longing look at the note, Dave wandered off, leaving Mark alone with his thoughts.

The way his heart had leapt when he'd thought the caller might have been Beatrice, concerned him. His reaction to seeing her yesterday could be explained by the unexpectedness of the encounter. But today...?

He should definitely leave. Who was it who'd said that the past was a country one should never revisit? He couldn't remember, but the sentiment was spot on. Picklewick had been magical growing up. It wasn't quite as magical now that he was an adult and viewing it through adult eyes. It was still pretty and quaint, and still unspoilt, but it wasn't doing anything for him.

Not wanting to be rude, or offend his readership (the adult contingent, that is), after Mark finished his lunch he gave Nikki Warring a call.

'Mr Stafford! Thank you so much for getting back to me,' she said. 'I'm Dulcie's sister. I wish I'd known at the time that it was you who had stepped into the breach on Saturday – I would have loved to have met you. Actually, that's what I wanted to speak to you about. I teach at Picklewick Primary and I wondered whether you could be persuaded to visit our school? The children would be thrilled to bits if you did.' She paused for breath.

Seeing an opening, Mark leapt in. 'I'd love to, but I doubt I'm going to be in Picklewick long.'

'It won't take long. Just an hour of your time. Please? We don't often get many authors in this neck of the woods, and to think you went to this very school.'

And that was how Mark Stafford, successful children's author (hopefully dressed in his own clothes this time) agreed to visit Picklewick Primary School on Wednesday afternoon to entertain small children for the second time in less than a week.

Beatrice couldn't believe how quickly time could speed by. No sooner did she arrive at the farm shop, than it was time to leave to collect the girls from school. She was thoroughly enjoying every minute of her new job, and every day was different.

She assumed things would probably settle down after Christmas, but for now she was rushed off her feet. Today, for instance, she'd been taste-testing milkshakes (mince pie flavour had been her favourite) and putting together festive afternoon tea boxes. There had been a steady stream of customers, and she knew that as the weekend approached, it would get even busier.

It was only Wednesday but Beatrice was already looking forward to Saturday. If last week was anything to go by, this next one should be fun. She was secretly disappointed that Mark wouldn't be there, wearing the Grinch's outfit, but maybe that was a good thing because, despite how busy she was both during and outside of work, Mark had been a constant presence in her mind.

She was also looking forward to Sunday. Beatrice loved her girls with every cell in her body, but she rarely had a minute to herself, so she treasured the times when they were with their father. Eric didn't often have them for a whole day because he was a nurse in Thornton General, which meant he worked days, nights and weekends too. She was planning a pampering day, and she knew she was going to need it after the busy week.

Right now she was on her way to collect the girls from school and she just had enough time to drop the car off at home and walk the six minutes from her front door to the school gates.

A gaggle of people were gathered in the playground waiting for the doors to open and the children to pour out of their various classrooms, and Beatrice spotted her best friend Lisa making her way over.

Lisa was studying her. 'Have you heard? Mark's back.'

Quietly Beatrice replied, 'I heard.'

'How do you feel?' Lisa knew their history. How could she not, since she'd picked up the pieces. Beatrice had been a mess for a while.

She laughed, hoping it sounded natural. 'I'm fine. I've been over him for years. Mark Stafford is water under the bridge.'

'I heard a rumour that he was the farm's Grinch. That can't be right, can it?'

Airily Beatrice replied, 'I believe he was.'

'Have you seen him?'

'No.' It wasn't technically a lie. She hadn't seen **him** as such. She'd seen a green Grinchy mask.

'Do you think he'll have changed much?' Lisa asked.

Beatrice shrugged. 'No idea.'

'He looks the same in the photos of him online. Better, actually. More suave. Suaver.' Lisa flicked her wrist. 'You know what I mean.'

All Beatrice knew, was that she wished Lisa would change the subject. Mark had only been in Picklewick a few days and she was already heartily sick of hearing his name. She was certainly sick of thinking about him, especially since she suspected he hadn't given **her** a second thought since he'd left. And why would he? So what, if they'd dated once? It was a long time ago, and they'd hardly been in the same league as Romeo and Juliet. Well, **he** hadn't – she would have laid down her life for him. Once or twice she'd been tempted to tell him how she felt, but thankfully had been unable to find the courage – the devastation she'd felt when he ended their relationship had been bad enough, without adding the mortification of him knowing she was in love with him.

A bell rang and a second later children exploded from the various classroom doors, filling the playground with yells and screams, and a blur of movement.

Beatrice craned her neck to see Sadie, but the child was nowhere in sight. She caught a glimpse of Taya though, who was trying to play it cool by ignoring her.

'Oh, heck, what now?' she muttered, when she saw Miss Barnes signalling to her. 'Could you watch Taya for a minute?' she asked Lisa. 'I need to speak to Sadie's teacher.'

Lisa gave her a sympathetic smile.

'Can I have a quick word?' Miss Barnes asked.

Mutely, Beatrice nodded and followed the teacher into the classroom.

Sadie was sitting in one of the small chairs, her arms folded, her face mutinous.

Miss Barnes said, 'Sadie is a little upset today because she found out she's going to be a toadstool and not a fairy in the school play, and she's refusing to take part.'

Beatrice sighed. 'Leave it with me. She'll come around.' Maybe the pink sparkly fabric she had in mind would do the trick?

'Won't!' Sadie snapped. 'Toadstools are nasty.'

'Who says?'

'Everyone.'

Beatrice highly doubted that. 'Come on, let's get you home.' She held out a hand.

Sadie thrust her hands deeper into her armpits and stuck out her chin. 'No.'

'What do you mean **no**?'

'I'm not going until Miss says I can be a fairy.'

'In that case, you can stay here all night,' Beatrice said. Blackmail, even from a five-year-old, wasn't nice.

Miss Barnes said, 'We've had such a lovely afternoon, too. We've had a visit from an author, haven't we, Sadie? He spoke about your favourite book, didn't he? Look.' She pointed to the hallway. 'There he is. You don't want Mr Stafford to see you in a mood, do you?'

Beatrice froze, and her gaze was slowly drawn to the open classroom door and the hallway beyond. And she immediately locked eyes with him.

Recognition flared in his and a smile flitted across his face. He gave a small, awkward wave, then turned his attention back to Mrs Warring, Taya's teacher.

Irrationally, Beatrice wished she was wearing something more glamorous than jeans, boots and a padded jacket that made her look like a small hippo. The bobble hat with a red pompom on it wasn't her best look either, and neither was her make-up-free face. When all was said and done, she looked a mess.

Miss Barnes said, 'Excuse me a minute. I just want to say goodbye to Mr Stafford. He was so marvellous, and the children adored him.'

Beatrice dragged her gaze away and focused on her belligerent daughter. 'We're going,' she said, her tone brooking no argument.

'No.'

'If you don't do as you're told, you'll go straight to bed after tea, young lady.'

'Don't care.' Sadie settled herself more firmly in her chair.

'No TV and no games,' Beatrice warned.

Her daughter stared stubbornly straight ahead.

'No story,' Beatrice added, wondering what other sanctions she could impose.

Sadie shot her a glance, then hastily looked away.

Ah-ha! Leverage! 'In fact, I won't read you a bedtime story for the rest of the week, if you don't do as you're told.'

Sadie leapt to her feet and stamped her foot. 'I don't care! I won't be a toadstool. Toadstools are for boys.'

'Who says?'

Beatrice froze at the sound of Mark's voice. Great. Now he was a witness to her abysmal parenting skills as well as her frumpy, mumsy appearance.

Ignoring her, he walked up to Sadie. Sadie gazed up at him in awe, her defiance miraculously vanished.

Sitting in the chair next to the one Sadie had abruptly vacated, he reached into the inside of his coat and withdrew a small pad and a pencil. Wordlessly he flipped the pad open and began to draw.

Sadie glanced at Beatrice, who shrugged. She had no idea what was going on, either.

Mark's head was bowed, his attention on whatever it was he was doing, and Beatrice grabbed the opportunity to look at him properly.

Taller than her five-foot-six by at least half a foot, he had always been athletic, but he had filled out over the years, his shoulders broader than she remembered, tapering to a lean waist. His long legs were encased in black jeans, and he struggled to fold them underneath the low table.

His short, dark brown hair was longer on top, and had flashes of silver at the temples, and crow's feet crinkled at the corners of his hazel eyes, those same eyes that had haunted her dreams for many months after he'd broken it off with her. A dusting of stubble shadowed his jaw, and her gaze lingered on his lips until she forced herself to look away.

His fingers gripped the pencil, guiding it across the page with firm, deft strokes and in less than a minute, he'd finished.

Sadie let out a gasp when he tore out the page and gave it to her. 'It's me, Mummy. He drawed **me!**'

So he had. He'd drawn her little face peering out from a toadstool and she had a wand in her hand, with stars issuing from its tip.

'See?' he said. 'Toadstools aren't for boys. They're for girls, because they're magic. Without toadstools, fairies wouldn't be able to fly.'

The logic of that passed Beatrice by, but Sadie grasped it immediately.

'Fairy dust!' she exclaimed.

'Exactly!'

Her eyes narrowed, then she said to Beatrice, in a tone remarkably like that of a queen bestowing a favour, 'I think I **will** be a toadstool. A pink one, with a wand. Can I show Miss?' Without waiting for an answer, she trotted towards Miss Barnes's desk where the two teachers were examining some books.

As Beatrice watched her go, she felt Mark's eyes on her.

He said, 'She's cute.'

'She's a monster in little girl's clothing.'

He chuckled. 'She looks like you. They both do.'

'You make a good Grinch,' she countered.

'I'm not sure that's a compliment.'

Beatrice didn't say anything. He could take it whichever way he pleased.

Sadie appeared at her elbow. 'Can we go now? I'm hungry.'

'I think we'd better. Miss Barnes will want to go home.' She grabbed her daughter's hand and smiled at the teachers. 'Nice seeing you again, Mark,' she said, her voice cool and polite.

'Wait, have you got time for a coffee?'

Beatrice blinked. **He wanted to have coffee with her?** Was this for old time's sake?

'Can't. Sorry.' She gestured towards her daughter.

'Another time?'

'Another time,' she agreed.

'When?'

'Pardon?'

'When would be best for you?'

'Mummy, you could have coffee with Mr Stafford on Sunday, if you don't want to take me and Taya.' Sadie's expression was hopeful. 'But I don't mind going now though. I could have a milkshake, and I promise to be quiet if you want to talk grown-up things. Taya will be good too.'

'No, I—' Beatrice began.

'Sunday?' Mark said.

Sadie announced, 'We're going to Daddy's house.'

Beatrice closed her eyes briefly. Thanks, Sadie. 'I'm busy on Sunday,' she said.

'She's going to have a bath with bubbles, but it won't take all day, will it, Mummy?'

Mark was staring at her, and Beatrice squirmed.

With a weak laugh, she said, 'I look forward to a relaxing soak in the tub without kids knocking on the door every few seconds. You know how it is.'

'Actually, I don't. No kids.'

'Oh.'

'Sunday?'

'I'm not sure.' She was so tempted that it was almost a physical ache. But seeing him again would be so unwise.

'It's just a coffee, Bea.'

Oh, bugger! Now he was thinking that she was reading more into it than he'd meant. 'Okay, eleven o'clock in Blake's Cafe on the main street.'

'See you there.' He began to walk away, then paused. 'Bea?'

'Yes?'

'Nice hat.'

Shit. Shit, shit, shit.

Beatrice sank onto the sofa, put her mobile on speaker, and reached for the glass of dry white wine on the side table next to her. She didn't make a habit of drinking on her own, and never on a weeknight, but this evening she felt the need to break her own rule.

'He asked me to go for a coffee with him,' she said, then winced as Lisa screeched, **'He asked you out?'**

'That's not what I said. He didn't ask me out. He asked me to go for a coffee.'

'Same thing.'

'It's not the same thing. It'll be a quick catch-up with an old friend – not a date.'

'Old friend, my peachy backside! He was your boyfriend.'

'**Was** being the operative word. That was years ago.'

'You were in love with him.'

'I might have been, but I'm not now.'

'Why do you think he asked you out?'

Beatrice didn't see the point in correcting Lisa again on the date front; instead, she said, 'For old time's sake.'

'Just be careful that old times don't become **new** times.'

'I'm not that daft. Anyway, I've heard he won't be in Picklewick long.'

'It doesn't take long,' Lisa pointed out, then her voice softened. 'I don't want to see you hurt, that's all.'

'I won't be. It's just a coffee with an old friend,' she reiterated.

'You keep telling yourself that.'

'Don't worry, I will. I'm not going to let Mark Stafford into my heart a second time.'

'That's the problem,' Lisa said. 'I don't think he ever left it.'

And although Beatrice scoffed at the idea, she had a suspicion her friend was right. He **had** been her first love, and did first love ever truly die...?

CHAPTER FOUR

Mark hesitated outside the cafe. It hadn't changed much and seeing it brought back a rush of memories. It whispered of summer afternoons after school, drinking ice-cold Cola, and winter ones sipping marshmallow-topped hot chocolates. And many of them had been with Bea by his side. This cafe was the embodiment of his youth, his salad days as Shakespeare had so eloquently put it. He had been green in judgement, indeed. But wasn't everyone at that age?

As the memories flooded back, Mark wondered how good an idea it was to invite Beatrice for a coffee. She'd clearly been reluctant, and to be honest, he wasn't entirely sure why he'd asked her. It had been a spur-of-the-moment thing, his mouth freewheeling down the road before his brain was in gear.

'Get over yourself,' he muttered. This was merely a chat and a coffee with an old friend. What was the harm in that?

With a deep breath, he pushed the door open and went inside. The bell above tinkled as the rich aroma of roasted beans filled his nose. The cafe was surprisingly busy, and although he was a few minutes early, Beatrice was already waiting for him.

She sat at a table in the corner, as though she was hiding away, and was fiddling with a packet of sugar, her eyes downcast. Behind him, the bell jangled again, but she didn't look up until he reached the table and paused.

'Hey,' he said.

'Hi.' She didn't smile. Her eyes were huge, her lashes long and dark, and he realised she was wearing make-up.

'Have you ordered?' he asked.

'Not yet.'

'What can I get you? A hot chocolate?'

She nodded. 'With marshmallows?'

'Absolutely! You can't have hot chocolate without marshmallows.'

'No...' She trailed off, her attention returning to the packet of sugar.

As he went to the counter to order their drinks, he wondered whether she still took two in her tea. And he wondered what she'd done in the intervening years while he'd been away. Got married, had two kids, got divorced... What else? Was she happy?

'I got you extra marshmallows,' he told her, placing the drinks on the table.

'Thanks.' She picked up a spoon and ladled some into her mouth, along with a generous dollop of cream, and he tried not to stare.

How many times had he kissed those lips?

She noticed the direction of his gaze and he hastily examined his own mug. 'So,' he began. 'How have you been?'

'Fine. Good. Great, actually.'

'Good, good.' He used his spoon to poke one of the marshmallows. It disappeared into the cream. He did the same to another, silence stretching between them.

Beatrice broke it. 'How about you?'

Mark opened his mouth to say 'good', then changed his mind. 'I've been better.'

'Are you ill?' A flicker of concern crossed her face, and he wondered what it meant.

'God, no, nothing like that,' he said. 'The only thing I'm suffering from is writer's block.' As soon as the words left his mouth, he regretted them. He had told no one, not even his agent or his editor. **Especially** not his editor.

'Writer's block? Is that where you can't think of anything to write?'

'Exactly.'

'I thought that was why you're here – to write one? Dulcie told me you're doing research.'

'I am. Kind of. I'm searching for inspiration.'

'Have you found any?'

'Not yet. I'm sure I will.' He took a sip of his drink, hoping he didn't have a cream moustache.

Beatrice said, 'You've got...' She touched her upper lip.

Dabbing his mouth with a serviette, he said, 'Anyway, enough about me. Tell me about you.'

'There's nothing to tell.'

'You've got children,' he pointed out.

'So I have.'

'You don't live with their father?'

'Thanks, Sadie,' she mumbled, then louder, 'We're divorced. How about you? Are you married?'

'Not anymore.'

'Oh. Sorry.'

'Me, too.'

'What happened?' Her eyes widened then she said, 'Forgive me, it's none of my business.'

'I don't mind talking about it. She didn't want kids. I did. I think the last straw was when I gave up the day job to become a full-time author.' It was more complicated than that, but the details weren't particularly pleasant.

Beatrice pursed her lips. 'That's tough.'

'Your turn.'

'I didn't realise we were swapping divorce stories.'

He made a face. 'You don't have to tell me, if you don't want to.'

'My ex is an arse. And before you ask why I married an arse, he wasn't one when we tied the knot. He became an arse later, after we'd had the kids.'

'Oh, right.' Her reply was cryptic and Mark wondered what the man had done. 'He still sees the kids, though?'

'He does, when it suits him. But he's still an arse.'

'Okay, I get it – he's an arse.'

'A lot of men are.' She looked him in the eye as she said it.

Although hoping she wasn't including him in that, he thought it prudent to change the subject. 'How long have you worked at Lilac Tree Farm?'

'Just over a week.'

'What made you decide to take a job on a farm?'

'Because Christmas is coming and my children want the earth – like every other kid on the planet.'

'I didn't mean that; I meant that I didn't think you were the mucking-out-the-cows type'

'Ah, okay.' She looked embarrassed, like she'd given too much away. 'I'm not. I only work in the shop. No cows. Or any other animal for that matter. Although the goats are rather sweet and the bunnies are very cute, the nearest I get to an animal, is selling their milk, or when Peg pays me a visit.'

'Peg?'

'Walter's dog. He persuaded her to sit outside the Grinch's cave, wearing antlers. It's costing him an arm and a leg in bones to keep her quiet.'

'Not his own, I hope?' Mark quipped and got a glare of disapproval for his efforts.

'I wish children were more like dogs,' she said. 'Happy with the simple things. You don't see them queuing up to see a Doggy Santa Claus and asking for diamante collars or gold-plated tennis balls. All they want is someone to love them, a comfy place to sleep, and a regular supply of dog biscuits.'

Mark grinned. 'But if there was a Santa **Paws** – see what I did? – pooches would still ask for things like squirrels to chase or squeaky toys.'

Sighing, she said, 'I suppose you're right. Whatever we've got, we always want more, even when we've got more than enough for our needs.' She blinked. 'Crumbs, that was a bit deep.' She finished her hot chocolate and licked her lips. 'I'd better go,' she said, getting to her feet. 'Thanks for the drink and the chat. It was nice catching up.'

'It was. I'm glad you're doing okay, Bea.'

'Why wouldn't I be?' she shot back.

'You know, divorce… two kids…'

Her face cleared. 'Yeah. You, too. I'm sure something will come to you soon.'

It already had. 'We should do this again,' he said.

'Next time you're in Picklewick,' she agreed.

'I mean, before then. Next week, maybe?'

'I thought you were leaving soon?' She seemed put out.

'I was thinking about it, but I've changed my mind. We could have dinner in The Black Horse. I'm fed up with eating on my own.'

'You forget I have children.'

'I haven't forgotten at all. Bring them with you. We can eat early; is five-thirty okay? My treat.'

'I can pay my own way.'

Mark was taken aback. 'I didn't for one minute think you couldn't.' An idea occurred to him, though why he was so anxious for her to agree, he had yet to determine. 'Call it a business meeting. I want to pick your children's brains.'

'Why?' Her suspicion was palpable. She clearly didn't believe a word he was saying.

'I have an idea for the new book and I'd like to run it past them, so dinner will be a legitimate expense.' It wouldn't, but she didn't need to know that.

'I thought you had writer's block?'

'I did, but I don't now.' He smiled warmly at her. 'It's amazing what a chat with an old friend can do.'

'Less of the old.' Her reply was automatic and lacked conviction. She sighed. 'Okay – when?'

'I'll fit in with you and your plans.'

'Friday,' she said. 'I don't want the kids worked up on a school night.'

'Friday, it is.' He'd hoped it could be sooner, but he supposed five days would give him time to hone his idea and produce some illustrations to show her children, and then he wouldn't be making himself out to be a liar. Because the real reason he had asked her to dinner was that he simply wanted to see her again. But why that was, he wasn't prepared to think about too closely.

The front door banging open, accompanied by shouts of 'Mummy, why is it so dark?' jolted Beatrice out of her thoughts, and she leapt out of the chair and switched on the nearest lamp.

Sadie barrelled into her, smelling of Eric's cologne and bringing a blast of chilly air with her. 'I was scared you were out!'

'I'm not out, I'm here.'

'But it was dark. You don't like the dark.'

'**You** don't like the dark,' Beatrice corrected her youngest child. 'I don't mind it. Where's your sister?'

Sadie's expression clouded. 'She told Daddy she hates him. She doesn't, does she?'

'Of course she doesn't. I expect she was cross with him, that's all.' Beatrice moved to the window and peered into the street. She could see Taya in the passenger seat of Eric's car. It was parked under the street light, illuminating her face. Taya looked remarkably like Sadie when she was annoyed about something.

Eventually she got out and slammed the door. The car rocked.

No doubt she would tell Beatrice about it later. For now, Beatrice wanted to make them some tea.

The front door banged open a second time as Taya stormed in, and Beatrice hurried to close it before it slammed shut.

If this carried on, she would have to replace the damned thing, and she couldn't afford to do that. Did her kids *know* how much a new front door cost?

Beatrice scowled. Of course they didn't, and if they did, they wouldn't care.

Aware that she was being ridiculous (they were children for goodness' sake!) she peered into the street again, then gently closed the door, hoping Eric hadn't upset their eldest child too much.

Beatrice got the story out of Taya over tea. 'Have you fallen out with Dad?' she asked.

Taya narrowed her eyes at her sister. 'Tattletale.'

'I'm not!'

Beatrice hastened to soothe sibling angst. 'Don't blame Sadie. I could tell from the way you stormed into the house.'

When it came to her children, there was always some drama or another, most of it minor and fleeting in the grand scheme of things, but of gigantic importance at the time. Hopefully this was of the minor and fleeting variety.

'Dad has got a girlfriend,' Taya spat.

Beatrice frowned in irritation. 'Was she there? Did you meet her?'

'No, I heard them talking on the phone.'

'You shouldn't listen in on people's conversations,' Beatrice said absently, relieved that her children hadn't been subjected to yet another of Eric's girlfriends.

She wouldn't have any objection if there was a constant one, or even if he'd had two since they'd split up, but he seemed to have a different one every week. Where he found them was a mystery. In all that time, Beatrice had only managed one date. It hadn't been a great success. Maybe single eligible women were in greater abundance than single eligible men?

'She won't last,' Beatrice told her daughter confidently. 'They never do.'

Taya pouted. 'I told him **you** had a boyfriend.'

'You did **what?** Why?'

'You **said** he was your boyfriend.'

'Who?'

'That man who came to the school. The one who wrote those books.'

Beatrice couldn't believe what she was hearing. 'His name is Mark Stafford, but he's not my boyfriend. Whatever gave you that idea?'

'I heard you talking to Aunty Lisa.'

'What did I just tell you about listening to other people's conversations? The problem is, you get the wrong end of the stick, or only half a story. Mark used to be my boyfriend, years ago. Long before I met your dad.'

'Why did you go out with him today? Do you want him to be your boyfriend again?'

'It was a work thing.' Seeing Taya's confused expression, Beatrice explained,

'He's writing a new book and wanted to have a chat.'

'Why?'

'Because he wants to ask whether he could talk to you and Sadie about it.'

'Why?'

'Because he doesn't have any children of his own to ask. And before you ask why, I don't know.' She took a deep breath. 'I said we'd go out to tea with him on Friday.'

Sadie had been following the conversation closely. 'Me, too?'

'Yes, sweetie, you too.'

'Yay! Can I have a Big Mac?'

'We won't be going to McDonald's,' Beatrice told her. 'We're going to The Black Horse.'

Sadie's eyes were round, Taya's not so much. At nine, Taya was more worldly-wise than her sister.

'I like him,' Sadie announced. 'He draws good.'

'Draws well,' Beatrice corrected.

'That's what I said.'

Beatrice's gaze strayed to the fridge. The drawing that Mark had done of Sadie dressed as a toadstool had pride of place, alongside the artwork that Taya produced on a weekly basis. As well as being a reader, Taya was a budding artist.

It was time to change the subject. 'If you've finished your tea, scrape off your plates and clear the table, please.'

'Aww, do we—?'

'Yes. Please can we not do this every mealtime?'

'Dad lets us—'

'I'm not interested in what your father does,' Beatrice broke in. She **was,** but she wasn't going to sweat the small stuff. Arguing with him about little things like this, simply wasn't worth the aggro.

Taya said, 'He always asks me about **you**.'

The look on her eldest child's face squeezed her heart. 'Taya, sweetie, I know you'd love nothing more than for me and your dad to get back together, but it's not going to happen.'

'He's only got a girlfriend because he's lonely.'

Yeah, right, Beatrice scoffed silently. He must have been very sodding lonely when they were married, because he'd had two affairs that she knew of. How many more that she didn't?

One day her girls might discover the truth about their arse of a father, but they wouldn't hear it from her.

Taya continued. 'You've got us. He hasn't got anyone.'

Maybe Eric should have thought about that before he cheated on me, Beatrice thought. She'd forgiven him the first time, but not the second.

Telling him she wanted a divorce had been the second hardest thing she'd ever had to do. The hardest had been telling the children that their dad wouldn't be living with them anymore. Taya had been devastated. At not-quite-two years old, Sadie hadn't understood what was going on.

Now and again, Beatrice wondered whether she'd done the right thing, that maybe she should have turned a blind eye to his philandering for the sake of her girls. And although she'd done nothing wrong and nothing to be ashamed of, in the dark quiet hours guilt gnawed at her with sharp black teeth.

'Bugger, damn and blast!' The sodding car wouldn't start. Beatrice turned the key in the ignition again, hoping and praying the engine would turn over, but all she heard was a defiant click. Why did it have to break down when it was raining? Sod's bloody law, that's what it was. It hadn't been raining when she'd taken the girls to school, but as she'd trotted back to the house to pick up the car and drive to work, the heavens had opened.

Thankfully she'd had an umbrella in her bag so she hadn't got too soaked. It had been buried underneath the spare hair bobbles, the Calpol sachets, the plasters and everything else she carried around with her **just in case**, because, let's face it, if she didn't have it, she would wish she did (Mary Bloody Poppins, that's who she was). However, umbrella or not, she would soon be drenched if she had to walk all the way from the village to the farm at the top of Muddypuddle Lane.

She tried the key again. Nothing.

Initially, when she'd got in the car, the hem of her jeans wet, the umbrella dripping, the engine had kind of turned over, making a chugging sound as it tried to fire – or whatever it was that engines were supposed to do – but that quickly became an asthmatic wheeze, and now it was refusing to do anything other than click. She had a feeling it was giving her the finger.

Cross, she began phoning people in the hope that one of them would be able to give her a lift. First her mum, then her dad, then Lisa…. As she worked her way down her contact list, becoming more despondent with every unanswered call or 'sorry, I would but—' she finally realised that the only way she was going to get to work was if she walked.

Whilst she'd been cursing the car (although she had a feeling that the car not starting was all her own fault, because she'd left the headlights on yesterday), the rain had eased and the clouds were beginning to clear. Hopefully it would stay fine for the next half an hour. She'd have to get a move on though, if she didn't want to be late, and she knew she was cutting it fine.

As she walked along the high street, she tried Dulcie's number, wanting to make her aware that she might be a few minutes late, but the call went straight to answerphone. As did her next call, which was to the garage.

'Fiddlesticks! Isn't **anyone** going to answer the phone this morning?' she grumbled.

'Everything okay?'

Beatrice froze and her heart sank. Great, that was all she needed. 'Mark, hi.'

He was outside the odds-and-sods shop, about to go in. 'Are you alright?' he asked. 'You look flustered.'

Gee, thanks for the compliment. 'I'm fine. I haven't got time to chat, I'll be late for work.'

'Oh, okay. See you tomorrow.'

Her phone rang. It was her dad. 'Sorry, I need to take this,' she said to Mark as she walked away. 'Hi, Dad.'

'What's up?' Her father's voice was full of concern.

'Nothing's wrong, but I need a lift to work. My car won't start.'

'Sorry, Bea, but your mum and I are in Thornbury.'

Beatrice sighed. 'Never mind. I'll speak to you later. Thanks anyway, Dad.'

'I can give you a lift, if you like?' Mark said.

Beatrice knitted her brow. She hadn't realised he had fallen in step with her until he'd spoken. 'Haven't you got anything better to do?' she asked.

His expression was blank when he replied, 'Actually, I have,' and stopped, turning away.

Realising how rude she'd been, Beatrice caught hold of his arm. 'I'm sorry, that came out wrong. If you're not busy, I'd love a lift, please.'

He glanced at her hand. Beatrice hastily removed it from his arm and dug her nails into her palm. Touching him had unsettled her. Meeting his gaze, she felt herself blush, but she couldn't look away.

'My car is in the pub's car park,' he said. 'Come on.' He strode off and she had to hurry to keep up.

The short walk was conducted in silence, and when she got into his rather smart black car she felt distinctly awkward.

Mark broke the silence as he reversed out of the parking space. 'Have you got a garage you can call?'

'There's one on the outskirts of Picklewick, but I'll see if Dad's got some jump leads first. I've got a feeling I need a new battery, but if I can get it going, it'll save me having it towed.'

'How will you get home?'

'Walk, probably.'

He signalled to turn right, then pulled onto the main road. They should be at the farm in five minutes.

He said, 'I'll fetch you. What time do you finish?'

'There's no need, honestly,' she replied, then subsided when a gust of wind buffeted the car. The heavens opened once more and the windscreen wipers went into overdrive.

'Three o'clock,' she told him, gratefully.

But when he dropped her off in the farmyard, she feared she had made a mistake and that walking would be preferable after all – despite the risk of a good soaking. Because the risk of being hurt again by this man grew every time she clapped eyes on him.

Muddypuddle Lane was narrow, with room for only one vehicle at a time, apart from the two passing places. One of those was the entrance to the stables, the other was outside a pretty cottage halfway up.

Mark was on his way to fetch Beatrice from the farm, when he spied another vehicle coming down the lane, so he pulled in next to the cottage. And wished he hadn't when Dulcie pulled up alongside and waved at him.

It wasn't a 'hello' kind of wave: it was more of a 'can I have a word' kind of wave, and the word she wanted concerned a certain green costume and small children.

'Please,' she begged. 'Walter isn't up to it, and Gio – that's Nikki's other half – was supposed to be doing it, but he's having to work on Saturday. I hate to ask, but you were **such** a big hit. I'd do it myself, but I'm running a pinecone decorating session. It'll only be for a couple of hours. **Please?**'

He hesitated, and her face fell.

'I shouldn't have asked. Note to self – be more organised next year. This is my first year doing a Christmas Wonderland, so I didn't know what to expect. I can't believe how well it's taken off.' She brightened. 'I'm not complaining, you understand.'

Against his better judgement, he said, 'Okay, I'll do it.'

'You **will?** That's marvellous. Thank you!' She looked so pleased that Mark was glad he'd agreed.

What was a couple of hours out of his day?

Dulcie said, 'This time I insist on paying you,' and when he shook his head, she said, 'Dinner at The Wild Side, then? Just let me know when and for how many.'

'It'll just be me,' he said.

'Why not ask Beatrice if you don't want to dine on your own?' Dulcie's expression was devoid of guile, but he couldn't shake the feeling he was being set up. It occurred to him that her sister Nikki must have overheard him asking Beatrice to have a coffee with him when he was at the primary school the other day. Either that, or they had been spotted in the cafe – which was also quite likely.

Beatrice was waiting when Mark drove into the yard, and she hopped into the car. 'Thanks for this. I really appreciate it.'

'It's no bother,' he replied, trying not to stare at the silver glitter on her nose. 'You've got, um...' He touched his own nose, and she pulled down the sun visor and examined her face in the mirror.

Laughing, she said, 'I've been making up Christmas Eve boxes – or as much as can be done ahead of time. Can't add the perishables just yet. That'll be a last-minute job. Did you know that there's such a thing as edible glitter?' She rubbed her nose, transferring the glitter to her finger, then popped it into her mouth.

When she stuck out her tongue, it was sparkly.

'I didn't,' he replied. 'Thanks for enlightening me. That's one piece of knowledge I don't know how I've survived without.'

She beamed at him. 'Every day is a school day,' she sing-songed.

'I've got a present for you. It's on the back seat.'

Her smile dimmed, her expression becoming wary. 'What is it?'

'Take a look.' Mark watched her out of the corner of his eye as she wriggled around and reached behind her.

When she opened the bag and saw what was inside, she burst out laughing. 'Who says romance isn't dead!' she cried, holding a set of jump leads aloft. Then her eyes widened, her mouth became an 'O' of dismay, and she blushed furiously. 'I didn't— Oh, bugger!'

Mark barked out a laugh, quickly sobering when she glared at him. He wasn't entirely certain which of them had what end of the stick. He clearly hadn't meant the jump leads to be any kind of romantic overture – what bloke in his right mind would give a woman a garage-related gift if he was trying to woo her? But did she think that was what he was trying to do – woo her? Or had she been hoping that the bag had contained something a little less practical?

'Do you know how to jump-start a car?' he asked, thinking he'd better steer the conversation into less emotionally turbulent waters.

But his plan backfired when she rolled her eyes and gave an exasperated sigh. 'Yes, I **do** know how to jump-start a car. I'm not completely inept.'

Gritting his teeth, he asked, 'Where do you live?'

'Lavender Lane, number four, but do you mind dropping me at the school instead?'

'Not at all.' His voice was stiff and stilted, and without saying another word he drove along the high street, reaching the school a minute later.

'Thanks,' she said, unclipping her seat belt. Then she held up the bag. 'Thanks for these, too.' She got out.

Without thinking, he said, 'I'll wait for you.'

'Why?'

'I'll take you home, and you can use my car to start yours.'

'Oh, right, thanks. That's very kind of you. Can I meet you there? You don't have any booster seats, and I know it's not far, but....'

'No problem.' **Booster seats?** He clearly had a lot to learn when it came to kids.

Mark watched her walk through the school gates, then realised he was getting curious looks from some of the mums, so he hastily drove off.

Waiting outside Beatrice's house, it felt like ages before she appeared with the children in tow, but it couldn't have been more than ten minutes.

'I'll be with you in a sec,' she said, unlocking the door to number four, a neat, terraced house with an old banger of a car parked outside, which he assumed was hers.

She ushered the children inside, then hurried back out, looking flustered.

'Problem?' he asked, flipping the lever to open the bonnet, then getting out.

'Nosey children.'

Movement caught his eye, and he glanced at the window to see two small faces peering out. Tentatively he waved and Sadie, the youngest, waved back. The older one glowered and he assumed she wasn't a fan, too old for books aimed at four- to seven-year-olds.

Beatrice popped the bonnet on her car, but before she was able to connect the leads to the battery, Sadie came outside. 'I've got a tummy ache,' the child announced.

'Is it because you're hungry?' Beatrice asked. She said to him, 'I think she's been confusing hunger pangs for tummy ache lately.'

'Give me your keys,' he said. 'I know you're perfectly capable of jump-starting a car, but you're probably better off seeing to the girls while I get this going. It'll take a while to transfer enough charge, and then you'll have to take it for a drive.'

'Damn, I'd forgotten that. Oh, well, I could do with getting a few things, so we'll pop into Thornbury. The kids can have a McDonald's on the way back as a treat.'

Sadie's ears pricked up. 'McDonald's? Really?' She jumped up and down, flapping her arms. 'Yay! McDonald's!'

Beatrice said, 'Anyone would think I never fed them. Actually, they don't have fast food often, so maybe it is something to get excited about. For them, not me, you understand.' She handed him her keys and went back inside, her bouncy, excited daughter racing ahead of her.

After fifteen minutes or so of the car being on charge, he disconnected the leads then tried it again. Reluctantly, it coughed into life, so he left it running, just in case, and knocked on her door.

'All done,' he said, stepping back when Sadie shot out and threw herself at him.

'Thank you!' she cried. 'Mummy said we've got you to thank for going to McDonald's. So that's what I'm doing, saying thank you.'

Mark met Beatrice's gaze over the top of her daughter's head. 'Thanks from me, too,' she said.

'No problem.'

'Can Mr Stafford come with us, Mummy?' Sadie released him and looked hopefully up at her mother.

Seeing the alarm in Beatrice's eyes, Mark said, 'Sorry, Sadie, I'd love to but I can't.'

Beatrice didn't try to persuade him to change his mind but as he drove off, he wished she had. There was nothing Mark would have loved more right now, than to eat a burger and fries with Beatrice and her children.

CHAPTER FIVE

Beatrice held the pub door open for the girls and in they went, wide-eyed and shedding hats and scarves as the warmth hit them. It was only a short walk from their house to The Black Horse, but it was dark and cold outside, with a chill north-easterly wind, so she'd made sure they were dressed warmly – they would need the layers on the way home.

The children hesitated inside the door, the pub unfamiliar and overwhelming. Beatrice also paused as she took in the Christmas tree in the corner, the multicoloured lights strung around the windows, and the twinkling, flashing garland festooned across the mantlepiece. Flames leapt in the log burner, and along with the smell of food and hops, there was a hint of woodsmoke and pine in the air.

Scanning the tables, she spotted Mark and some of the tension she had been carrying eased.

From behind the bar, Dave waved at her and she gave him a fleeting smile as she shepherded the girls past, feeling awkward. She wasn't a weekly visitor to The Black Horse, but she drank there often enough not to feel discomforted that she was here to meet a man. This was her local, for goodness' sake – she'd had her first legal drink in this very pub (and her first illegal one, too), but this evening, she felt as though she'd walked into a strange bar and everyone was staring at her.

Actually, quite a few people **were**, and she knew all of them, including Dulcie and her younger sister Maisie, who had recently opened a boarding kennels on the mountain above the farm. When Dulcie saw whose table Beatrice was heading towards, she smirked and raised her eyebrows.

Beatrice stuck her nose in the air and fixed her gaze on Mark – which was a mistake, as she felt her cheeks pinking up, especially when he got to his feet and went in for a hug. The contact was brief, but it set her nerves jangling nevertheless as her body remembered what it was like to be held by him.

Heat flooded through her and she hastily shrugged out of her coat.

'Sit down, girls,' she instructed, folding it over her arm as she pulled out a chair for Sadie. Sadie ignored it and sat next to Mark. Taya sat next to her sister, leaving one unoccupied seat on Mark's other side.

Sadie shuffled her chair closer to him. Ironically Beatrice moved her own chair further away; not by much, but enough to give her a little more space to breathe. Right now, it felt as though there wasn't enough air in the room. Or was that due to the heat the log burner was spewing out?

Yes, that was it. Probably.

Sadie had begun chatting away as soon as she'd sat down, but Taya was more reserved and hadn't said a word, and Beatrice had the impression that her eldest child wasn't as keen on Mark as her youngest was.

It took a while to choose their meals, mainly because Sadie couldn't decide, but with the food eventually ordered, Mark settled down to business. Taking a digital tablet out of its fabric sleeve, he proceeded to discuss his idea with the girls, and both were fascinated with the artwork he'd done so far, Taya especially, who was emerging from her shell now that she had something electronic to focus on.

'I assumed you used paper and paint,' Beatrice said.

'I do, but digital art is less messy, and because digital lets me layer my work, if I want to change something, the colour of the dog let's say, then I can do so easily without having to repaint the whole thing.'

'Can I have a go?' Taya asked. She hadn't taken her eyes off the screen.

Mark said, 'You can, but on one condition – you give me your honest opinion about the story. I know it isn't aimed at someone your age, but your input is still valuable. Yours, too, Bea; as a parent.'

By the time their meals arrived, Mark's idea for his new book had been thoroughly discussed, and Taya had become totally enthralled with digital art.

'Can I have a tablet, Mum?' she asked.

Beatrice's heart sank; she'd been expecting her daughter to ask, but she was hoping she wouldn't. Tablets like this weren't cheap. Even with her new job at the farm, she was pretty sure she couldn't afford to buy one, especially with Christmas being only a few weeks away and she'd already begun buying gifts, not wanting to leave everything to the last minute.

Maybe if she had a word with their father? It was about time Eric pulled out his wallet.

'We'll see,' Beatrice told her.

'I won't ask for anything else ever again,' Taya promised earnestly.

Beatrice highly doubted that.

'Look what it can do, Mum.' Taya angled the screen so Beatrice could see.

Mark said, 'It's only a tool, Taya. **It** didn't create that – **you** did.'

Beatrice studied the image, pride swelling in her chest. Although she knew Taya was good at drawing and painting, until she saw what she'd created on Mark's tablet in a matter of minutes, Beatrice hadn't realised just how good. Taya appeared to have found her niche.

But was it just a fad? It was a lot of money to spend on something if it wasn't going to be used.

Mark put the tablet away while they ate and didn't bring it out again, which Beatrice was thankful for, and the conversation moved on from book writing and digital art. By the time they were ready to order dessert, they were discussing weird food combinations.

'Ice cream and chips!' Sadie cried.

Mark pretended to think about it. 'Do you know, I think that might be quite nice. How about popcorn and tomato sauce?'

'Gross!'

'Bacon and chocolate?'

'Ew!

'Pineapple and pizza?' he suggested.

Taya narrowed her eyes. 'Duh, that's a real thing.'

'No! It can't be!' Mark looked shocked, but Beatrice caught the twinkle in his eye.

'It's called a Hawaiian,' Taya said. '**Everyone** knows that.'

Sadie wrinkled her nose. 'It's yucky.'

Beatrice was inclined to agree with her, but ham and pineapple was Taya's favourite pizza topping.

'Haribo and porridge,' Sadie suggested.

Mark tapped his chin. 'Does your Mum make porridge in the microwave?' he asked, and when Sadie nodded he said, 'Would you put the Haribo in first, so they went all melty, or after the porridge is cooked?'

'**All melty?**' Beatrice laughed. 'Melty isn't a word.'

'It is. It's a made-up word. Us authors are allowed to make up words,' he replied loftily. 'Ask Lewis Carroll.'

'Who's Lewis Carroll?' Taya wanted to know.

Mark said, 'He wrote Alice's Adventures in Wonderland.'

'That's a film, not a book,' she told him.

'It was a book before it became a film. Lewis Carroll wrote it over a hundred and fifty years ago.'

'Is he dead?' Sadie asked.

'Very.'

'Then how can you ask him about made-up words?' Sadie looked confused.

'You can't, but he wrote a poem called The Jabberwocky and it's full of them.' And to Beatrice's astonishment, he recited the whole poem whilst the children ate their chocolate sundaes and she sipped her coffee.

The kids were enthralled, despite not understanding most of it and when he finished, she gave him a round of applause and he gave a mock bow.

'Bravo!' she cried, impressed.

In fact, she'd been impressed all evening by how good he was with the children, and she thought it such a pity he didn't have any of his own – he would make a great dad.

When Sadie started to yawn and Beatrice announced it was time to go, he insisted on walking them home, despite her protestations of it not being far.

As the girls trotted ahead, the adults followed at a more sedate pace. It felt surreal to Beatrice. How many times had she walked along this very street with him, their arms around each other's waists or holding hands? It was almost as though she'd gone back twenty years, and she had to stop herself reaching out to take his hand.

Beatrice shivered, but not from the cold. It was from a longing so intense that it stole her breath.

You can't turn back time, she told herself.

But it wasn't a longing for the girl she'd once been and the life she had yet to lead that was making her feel this way — it was **Mark**.

Sadie's giggle broke into her thoughts, and she brushed them away. It didn't do to dwell on the past and no good ever came of it. Anyway, it wasn't as though she could have changed anything. Even if she had told him she loved him, he still would have left, and she still would have been dumped. The only difference was that she would have had a generous dollop of humiliation to go with her heartbreak.

'I think they enjoyed themselves, judging by the amount of food they packed away,' she said, trying to rein in her wayward thoughts. 'Thank you for inviting us.'

'I did have an ulterior motive, if you remember.' His shoulder brushed against hers as he dodged around a lamp post with a flashing snowman at the top of it.

'I don't think Taya will allow me to forget. She was quite taken with your tablet.'

'There are cheaper options on the market, ones that will do roughly the same job,' he said quietly.

'That's good to know.'

'Do you want me to send you some links?'

'It wouldn't hurt to take a look,' she replied, thinking that Mark's version of cheap mightn't be the same as hers. Maybe if she and her parents clubbed together, they could buy Taya one between them?

Beatrice came to an awkward halt outside her house, wishing he hadn't insisted on walking her home. Even with the children present, it felt too much like a date, and she hoped he wasn't expecting to come in.

She said, 'I'd better get Sadie into her PJs. If I don't put her to bed, she'll be fit for nothing tomorrow.'

'Speaking of tomorrow, Dulcie has roped me into playing the Grinch again. I can't believe I let her do that.'

'Green suits you.'

'Why do I get the feeling that's not a compliment? See you at the farm tomorrow, Bea. Bye, girls.'

And with that he was off, striding back along the street, leaving Beatrice standing on her doorstep, wishing that she had asked him in after all.

The evening was still young so Mark had two options: sit in his room and watch TV, or return to the bar and people-watch. He chose the latter.

Perching on a stool, he ordered a pint and took out his mobile. After a bit of scrolling, he found what he was looking for and pinged off the promised links to

Beatrice, then he leant against the counter and tried to marshal his thoughts.

He'd done what he'd set out to do in coming here; Picklewick had well and truly got his creative juices flowing, and although there was a great deal of flesh to be put on his new book, the bones of it were there. The artwork was rough and the story a ghost of what it would eventually be, but the hardest part, the premise – which was what he had been struggling with – was done.

He needn't stay in Picklewick any longer. He could return home, where it would be far more comfortable and much less expensive. Nothing was keeping him here, he had no reason to hang around.

However, an image of Beatrice flashed into his mind and it gave him pause. But only for a moment and then he pushed it away. Even if he did stand a chance with her, he wouldn't try. It wouldn't be fair on either of them. She was firmly rooted in Picklewick and he lived in Bristol.

He would keep his promise to Dulcie to play the Grinch tomorrow, then he'd head off home.

Decision made, he took a long draught of his beer, almost spilling it down himself when a woman bumped his elbow.

'Oops, sorry,' she began, then recognition flashed in her eyes and Mark realised he knew her. 'Mark Stafford,' she said. 'Well I never! I'd heard you were in town.'

'Lisa Spencer, you haven't changed a bit.'

'Liar, but thank you anyway. And it's Lisa Edwards now.'

'How are you?'

'I've got three kids, a husband with a broken arm, two dogs, a hamster, and a full-time job, so I think 'frazzled' is a good description.'

'Wow! That's a handful. I still think of you as being, like, twenty. It's a shock to see you all grown up, a real responsible adult.'

'I'm faking it. I don't feel in the least bit responsible or adult. Bea and I were saying that very thing the other day. Now, there's a lady who **definitely** hasn't changed much, don't you think?'

'She hasn't,' he agreed. 'She hardly looks a day older than the last time I saw her.'

'Which was the day you dumped her.'

Ouch. 'It might have been. I honestly don't remember.'

'I do. So does Bea.'

Where was Lisa going with this? There had been a lifetime of water under that particular bridge.

'Why are you here, Mark?' she asked, and he frowned. It was none of her business.

She carried on, 'Bea told me that you're writing a book, but surely you can do that anywhere? It doesn't have to be in Picklewick.'

That was out of line, so he felt he could also be blunt. 'What's it to you?'

'I picked up the pieces last time. I don't want to see her hurt again.'

'What pieces? What do you mean?'

Her eyes widened and she bit her lip. 'Nothing. Ignore me. Honestly, I don't know what I'm talking about.'

He wasn't going to let it drop. 'Are you saying I hurt her? I didn't think she was that into me. I mean, we dated for a few months but we weren't in love, or anything.' Actually, maybe he had been – a little. But **she** hadn't.

'Ten months and three weeks,' Lisa shot back. 'And Bea **was** in love with you.'

Mark blew out his cheeks. 'I didn't know.' Bloody hell. Was Lisa telling the truth?'

'Would it have made any difference?' Lisa asked.

'No. Maybe.' He thought again. 'I honestly don't know. I was young, ambitious. Hungry.' Would love have been enough to keep him in Picklewick? He would never know.

Lisa said, 'What are you now? Are you still ambitious?'

'Not as much,' he admitted.

She pursed her lips. 'Look, forget I said anything. Bea will kill me if she found out I told you.'

'So why did you?'

She shrugged, as though she wasn't sure herself. 'She's been through a lot lately.'

'The ex-husband?'

Lisa nodded. 'He cheated on her — twice.'

Mark experienced a surge of anger on Beatrice's behalf. Beatrice was right, her ex **was** an arse. He said, 'I don't believe there's any chance of her being hurt again. I think she's well and truly over me by now, don't you?'

'Yes, you're right, of course she is. I'm being silly.'

'You're looking out for her, that's all. It's what good friends do. You two go back a long way.'

'We do.' She glanced over her shoulder. 'I'd better go. My husband will be wondering where I've got to. I only came to the bar for a packet of salt and vinegar crisps. Nice seeing you again, Mark.'

'You, too.' He noticed that she left without buying a packet. Had she decided she didn't want any after all? Or had the crisps merely been an excuse to speak to him?

He finished his pint and ordered another, and as he leant against the counter and sipped it, he thought about what Lisa said. If Beatrice had been in love with him and she had been hurt when he ended their relationship, it might explain her initial frostiness towards him, although she'd thawed somewhat since.

But why had Lisa felt the need to say anything now? It was ancient history.

Or was it?

Mark loved those moments of inspiration or insight when ideas sprang into his mind, whether they be for a story or an article. When he'd been a journalist, he used to be pretty good at joining the dots, at seeing connections. It was sometimes described as a lightbulb moment, and he was having one of those moments **right now**.

Beatrice hadn't just been in love with him back then – she still **was** in love with him. Or so Lisa believed. Mark wasn't entirely convinced he'd arrived at the correct conclusion, but if anyone knew Beatrice's heart, it would be Lisa.

She was warning him off because she didn't want Beatrice to be hurt again. And that could only happen if Beatrice still had feelings for him.

Mark straightened up in shock. This could change everything.

The mask wasn't the most pleasant thing to wear, and two hours was all Mark could manage in one go. Thankfully he didn't have to play the Grinch for longer than that, as Dulcie was taking over from him as soon as she was done decorating pinecones.

She arrived, flustered but looking happy, wearing her elf outfit and carrying another Grinch costume in a bag. 'The one you're wearing is too big for me,' she explained, pulling it out and stepping into it.

Mark took his mask off with relief. 'That's better. I can breathe again.' He held it aloft. 'What do you want me to do with it?

'Can you turn it inside out and pop it in the bag? I'll clean it later, before the next poor sod has to wear it. I'm beginning to think I should have plumped for a regular Santa Claus costume, but the Grinch seemed like a good idea at the time.'

'He appears to be quite popular,' Mark said. 'The children love him.'

Dulcie beamed widely before putting on her own mask. 'They do, don't they? Right, time to get into character. Thanks again for helping out, and don't forget I owe you a meal at The Wild Side.'

Mark hadn't forgotten.

He left Dulcie to it and strolled across the yard, drawn towards "Otto's Christmas Kitchen" as the food area was called, by the tantalising smells issuing from it and his rumbling tummy.

The doors were open and framed by thick garlands which were dotted with red ribbons and gold-painted pinecones. Inside was equally as festive, with centrepieces of twinkling lanterns surrounded by a woven ring of holly and ivy on each of the picnic benches. Mark had come to expect fairy lights, and he wasn't disappointed because they were everywhere, strung from the rafters and draped around hay bales, and there was yet another Christmas tree just inside the door. The red and green plaid blankets were a lovely touch.

Dulcie had thought of everything.

Mark queued for a bowl of pumpkin soup topped with roasted chorizo, and a hunk of sourdough bread, and devoured it quickly. It was so good that he briefly considered going for seconds, but that would be greedy. Licking his fingers, he scrunched up the paper napkin and popped it in the bin, then blew out his cheeks.

As he was plucking up the courage to go see Beatrice to ask if she would have dinner at The Wild Side with him, he noticed a woman staring.

She smiled and walked towards him. 'Are you Mark Stafford? I'm Grace Daley.' She thrust out a hand. 'I'm a reporter with The Picklewick Paper.'

'Gosh! Is that still going?' He'd forgotten about that. Taking her hand, he shook it.

'It is, although we've had to change with the times. May I ask you a few questions?'

'It depends on what they are,' he replied warily. Reporters, as he was all too aware, needed to be treated with the same degree of caution as a microphone – always assume that anything you said could potentially appear in a tabloid somewhere, or in the case of a mic, be broadcast to all and sundry.

'Nothing controversial,' she assured him. 'Just about your books, where you get your inspiration, what you're working on now... That kind of thing. Can I buy you a coffee?'

Mark was used to interviews, having done several over the years and, as his agent kept stressing to him, getting his name out there was part and parcel of being an author. 'Books don't publicise themselves,' she was fond of saying.

'How about I buy **you** one?' he suggested, guiding her towards a free picnic table. 'They do some incredibly festive flavours.'

She chose a chestnut praline latte and although he was tempted by the chestnut syrup, whipped cream and caramel drizzle (it smelled divine), he opted for an orange espresso spiced with cinnamon, cloves and nutmeg.

When they had their drinks, Grace proceeded to ask him all the usual sorts of questions that he'd come to expect, and he answered them readily enough, even the ones about growing up in Picklewick, which were a little more personal than he liked. He tended not to respond to those, deeming that his private life should be, well, **private.**

But as they were about to wrap it up, the reporter asked a question that Mark didn't find as easy to answer, when she said, 'Where next after Picklewick?'

'Home,' he replied automatically.

But as the word passed his lips, he wondered where 'home' was, because for some reason Bristol no longer felt like it.

Beatrice was surprised to see him, and Mark wondered whether she'd forgotten he would be at the farm today.

She sent him a little smile, before turning her attention back to the customer she was serving, and while Mark waited for her to finish, he explored the shop. It wasn't very big, but it had a variety of items for sale, from foodstuff to soaps and candles. He was sorely tempted to buy a carton of that wonderful pumpkin soup, and if he had a way of reheating it, he would have done.

The place seemed to be doing a roaring trade and as more customers piled in, he wondered whether he would get a chance to speak to Beatrice in private.

Should he message her instead? If he did, the rejection he would invariably receive might be easier to deal with if she wasn't watching his face while she said it. Conversely though, she might be less inclined to say no if she **did** see his face, and by springing it on her now, she mightn't have a chance to think of an excuse.

It wasn't that he was desperate to take her out for a meal, but he **was** desperate to talk to her on her own, so doing it over a meal in a posh restaurant was better than having a drink in The Black Horse where every man and his dog might overhear.

Mark lingered for a while, picking things up and putting them down, and every so often when she'd finished serving one customer and before she started on the next, he'd try to have a conversation with her.

After several unsuccessful attempts, he realised that the only way he was going to speak to her was if he bought something, and even then he'd probably have to talk fast.

Mark looked longingly at the soup again, before picking up a gift box of handmade soaps. They looked like slices of cake, almost good enough to eat, and smelled lovely.

He took it to the counter. 'I thought my mother would like it,' he said, somewhat defensively in case she thought he was buying it for himself.

'Would you like it gift wrapped?'

'Yes, please.' Gift wrapping wouldn't take long, but he might need the additional time that the service would provide.

As she selected a length of pre-cut wrapping paper, he said, 'Dulcie isn't happy with me.'

She glanced up. 'Why is that?'

'I refused to take any payment for playing the Grinch.'

'That's kind of you.' She was frowning, and he hoped she didn't think he was telling her this just to show her what a nice guy he was.

'She feels really bad about it,' he added, watching her expertly fold the paper around the box. 'So I ended up accepting an offer of a meal in The Wild Side instead.'

'I've heard it's nice.' She used little gold stickers to keep the paper folds in place and reached for a ball of red string.

'You've not eaten there?'

She shook her head.

'The thing is,' he continued, 'I don't fancy going on my own. The meal is for two, so would you like to come with me?'

Beatrice was in the middle of tying the string into a bow, and she didn't look up.

He explained, 'I'm not going to go on my own. It's one thing eating a meal in The Black Horse on my tod, but in a posh place like The Wild Side, I'll look a real saddo.'

She popped the gift-wrapped parcel into a paper bag with the words Lilac Tree Farm written on it.

Mark held up his credit card, ready to pay. 'If you don't say yes, I'll tell Dulcie it's your fault that I won't be taking her up on her offer, and she can be cross with you instead.'

The look Beatrice gave him could have frozen mercury. 'When?'

'Whenever suits you.'

She rang his purchase up and handed him a receipt. 'I'll have to see if I can get a babysitter. Maybe Lisa could do it. You remember Lisa? We were best mates. We still are.'

He remembered Lisa all too well. 'What about your mum and dad?' he asked hurriedly. After his conversation with her last night, it might be better if Lisa didn't know about this – although he suspected she would get to hear of it at some point, whether Beatrice told her or via the local gossip mongers. But he hoped it would be after the meal, and not before it.

'I'll let you know,' she said, her attention already turning to the next customer. 'Thanks for the links, by the way.'

'Glad to help.' He smiled, but she didn't see it, and he left thinking that he mightn't hear from her again, or if he did it would be to tell him that she couldn't get a babysitter or that she'd changed her mind.

But he **did** hear from her, and when she suggested Tuesday, a huge grin spread across his face.

CHAPTER SIX

On Monday morning, Beatrice had her head in her wardrobe and was scrabbling around inside it hunting for her comfiest pair of jeans to wear to work, when Sadie appeared at her side.

'Mummy, I feel sick and I've got a tummy ache.' The plaintive note in her daughter's voice tugged at Beatrice's heartstrings.

Sadie's complaints of feeling sick were becoming a daily occurrence, usually when Beatrice was nagging the girls to get ready for school. She was beginning to fear that Sadie disliked school and was saying she felt ill in order to get out of going. However, she'd read somewhere that in young children mental distress could cause actual physical symptoms, so she wasn't about to accuse Sadie of making it up.

Sadie had loved nursery and she seemed to have settled into full-time school, but gradually, over the last few weeks – since October half term, in fact – she'd started to mention not feeling well. The usual culprits were feeling sick, and/or pain in her tummy. The symptoms didn't last long though, and Sadie more often than not perked up considerably by the time she arrived at school.

To Beatrice, it seemed as though Sadie disliked the **thought** of going to school, but didn't mind it when she was actually **there**.

Beatrice could sympathise with that. She used to feel the same about the exercise classes which she used to force herself to attend in the hope of staying slim and keeping fit. Maybe having a week off school at half term had disrupted Sadie and had made her decide she preferred being at home. Or perhaps something had happened at school that had upset her?

Beatrice crouched down beside her daughter, ignoring the nagging voice in her head reminding her that they were going to be late for school if she didn't get a move on. 'Where does it hurt?'

Sadie put a hand over her belly button. 'Here.'

'How sick do you feel?'

'Very.'

'Too sick to eat a biscuit?'

Sadie nodded.

Beatrice held out her arms and Sadie cuddled into her, saying, 'I won't be too sick for a biscuit in a minute.'

'Is that right?'

'Uh-huh. Has a minute passed yet?'

'No. How about you put your shoes on? That'll take a minute.' Beatrice didn't usually allow the girls biscuits this early in the day, but she was trying to gauge just how real the sicky tummy ache was.

'Do I have to go to school, Mummy? Can't I stay here with you?' Sadie asked, her face buried in Beatrice's neck. 'I promise I'll be good.'

'I won't be here, sweetie. I've got a job, remember? All the time you are in school, Mummy will be working in the shop at the farm.'

'I don't want you to.'

Bingo! **That** was it! It wasn't the change in routine brought about by the half term break that was the issue, it was Beatrice's new job. Maybe Sadie starting primary school and Beatrice going out to work for the first time in Sadie's young life, was proving to be too much too soon for her little daughter.

Reassured that there wasn't anything more serious troubling her child, and knowing that Sadie would soon get used to this new routine, Beatrice gave her a squeeze and stood up. 'Go put your shoes on and I'll get you a biscuit.'

'A Party Ring?' Sadie asked hopefully.

Beatrice had been thinking more along the lines of a plain Rich Tea, not a biscuit covered in lurid-coloured icing sugar.

'Don't push your luck,' she told her, relieved when Sadie bounced out of the bedroom, her tummy ache clearly gone.

Beatrice went back to her hunt for her jeans, and as she did so her attention was caught by the dress she'd bought in the sales last January and had never worn. Should she wear it to dinner with Mark? Black, figure-hugging to a certain degree, but not too much, and covered in a layer of black lace dotted with the occasional tiny diamante beads, it was both partyish and sophisticated – a typical LBD. But was it too over-the-top for a quiet dinner in a small restaurant with a man she shouldn't feel the need to impress?

This was **not** a date. She was doing him a favour and getting to enjoy a nice meal at the same time. As long as she didn't look like she'd just been cleaning out the chicken coop on the farm, did it matter what she wore? Mark wouldn't notice. So why did she feel this need to look her best?

'Mummy, I want my biscuit!' Sadie called, and Beatrice sighed.

She sighed again when Taya cried, 'Why does **she** get a biscuit and I don't? That's not fair!'

Grabbing the first pair of jeans she laid her hands on, Beatrice yanked them on, then went downstairs to distribute the biscuits before she had a full-blown mutiny on her hands.

'Mr Stafford? Mr Stafford!'

Mark halted in the middle of the pavement and glanced around. A plump middle-aged woman wearing a multicoloured voluminous coat and a pink knitted hat was waving frantically at him from the opposite side of the high street.

Mark had no idea who she was.

She darted across the road, and he winced when a car screeched to a halt as she stepped out in front of it. It missed her by a hair.

'It **is** Mark Stafford, isn't it?' she panted as she hurried towards him.

'It is,' he confirmed.

'Thank god. I'd feel awful accosting a total stranger.'

He didn't like to point out she was doing precisely that. 'Can I help you?'

'Oh, I do so hope you can. My class would love you.'

'I've already visited the school,' he said. Maybe she'd been off sick or on a course and had missed it.

'I know, that's why I wanted to talk to you. I hear you're a very amenable chap, very generous with your time.' She was trying to butter him up.

He said nothing and waited for her to continue, a polite smile on his face.

'I'm Melanie Parker and I run an art class at the community centre. We do all kinds, from watercolour to acrylic, landscapes to nudes, although it's probably best not to mention that, ha ha. Would you be kind enough to give a talk? A demonstration would be even better. I understand you do all your own illustrations.'

'I do, but I'm primarily a digital artist.'

'That's what I'd like you to talk about.' She leant in and lowered her voice. 'Some of them can't paint for toffee, bless them, so I was hoping they'd do better with an app.'

'Admittedly, it's a different skill set,' he replied, his voice guarded. App or not, he still had to draw the image, he still painted it: the only difference was the medium. Instead of paint and paper, he used a stylus and a screen. And he often perfected the initial drawing on paper first.

'I'm sure my students would be fascinated. They'll be interested to learn how you put a picture together.'

Mark wasn't sure what to say. He was used to giving interviews and talking about his books, and was used to going into schools and reading to the children. But this was the first time he had been asked to demonstrate the illustration side of his books.

He said, 'I'm not sure how it would work. I'd need an internet connection and an interactive whiteboard, so I can share my screen.'

Melanie Parker beamed at him. 'I'm sure we can cobble something together. Can you do tomorrow? We meet every Tuesday at two p.m. in the community centre. I'll be there from one thirty, setting up. Thanks ever so much. Toodle-oo.'

And that was how Mark Stafford, successful children's author, found himself trying to explain the ins and outs of digital art to a group of pensioners who thought the term 'graphic art' meant drawing people with no clothes on and appeared to be quite put out when they discovered it wasn't.

The coffee was mud-coloured and had a plasticky taste, but the Jammie Dodgers were nice. As biscuits went, it was one of his favourites. Mark helped himself to two.

Melanie said, 'I think that went well, don't you?'

'I'm not sure I've converted anyone.'

She laughed. 'Possibly not. The older you get, the more stuck in your ways you become. This lot – me included – grew up believing that drawing and painting involved pencils and paints. One or two might give it a go, though. But even so, I don't think I'm going to be out of a job any time soon. It's the next generation I worry about. Everything is electronic and digital these days – they won't know what a paintbrush is. Not when it comes to art. Houses still need to be painted. Although I wouldn't be surprised if somebody somewhere doesn't invent a way to digitally change the colour of your sitting room walls. Anyway, like I said, I think my students found it interesting. And thank you for signing my grandson's copy of **The Elephant Who Forgot**. I love the way all your books have a message. I think that's why they're so popular.' She paused for breath, and Mark took a deep one of his own.

Melanie was lovely, but she couldn't half talk!

She was off again. 'How is the new one coming along? I heard you'd come to Picklewick for a bit of peace and quiet to write it. I bet you haven't found the village as quiet as you'd like if that's the case, what with dressing up as the Grinch at the farm, visiting the school and now this.' She chuckled. 'I wonder what you'll get up to next? Helping with the nativity play at the stables? They have one every Christmas, you know. The old people love it.'

'Old people?' He had a worrying vision of a group of OAPs on horseback.

'Yes, the kids at the stables put on a play and the residents of Honeymead Care Home go every year to watch – the ones that can manage it, that is. They have a lovely time. And the ones that can't, are shown it via the internet, on the TV. The staff are ever so good. I should know because my mother is in there. Dementia. So sad. That's why **The Elephant Who Forgot** is so special. It helps Joey, that's my grandson, understand why his Gan-Gan doesn't know who he is sometimes.'

Mark smiled. 'Glad it's of help.' He hoped his next book would be as useful. They weren't just for entertainment: he wanted to help educate young minds, too.

'How are you enjoying being back in Picklewick?' she asked. 'I understand you grew up here. From what I can gather, it hasn't changed much. Mind you, villages like this don't, do they? That's their charm. I used to live in Thornbury, but I moved here a couple of years ago when I retired. You wouldn't believe it, but I'm busier now than I was when I was working. I've always loved art. Would have liked to do it full-time but it didn't pay the bills. Now I've retired, I can paint all day if I want. Apart from Tuesday afternoons, when I run this art class, and Mondays when I—'

'I'm sorry to interrupt but I've got to get back. A call with my editor.' Mark was fibbing, and he felt bad about that, especially when Melanie was so nice about it.

'Of course, I mustn't keep you. You're a busy man and you've been so generous with your time. Thank you, again.' She clasped her hands over her heart. 'We really appreciate it.'

Despite Melanie chewing his ear off at the end, Mark found he'd enjoyed giving the demonstration. They had been an enthusiastic and interested group, and had made him feel very welcome.

In fact, everyone he'd met in the village had been friendly and welcoming. He was beginning to wonder why he'd ever left!

Why was she so nervous? This was ridiculous. It was only a meal.

'You look nice, Mummy.'

'Thank you, sweetie.' Beatrice glanced at Sadie through the mirror and smiled.

'Are you going out with Aunty Lisa?'

'No, with Mark, the man who writes the books, the one who we had a meal with on Friday.'

'Is he your boyfriend?'

'No!' Realising she'd said that rather sharply, she smiled at her daughter again. 'He's not my boyfriend. I'm doing him a favour, that's all.'

'What kind of favour?'

'I'm having a meal with him in The Wild Side, that nice restaurant on the high street, because he doesn't want to eat dinner on his own.'

'Is he lonely?'

'Maybe.' Beatrice hadn't considered that.

'Doesn't he have any friends?'

'Not in Picklewick.'

'**We** can be his friends. He can eat dinner here, then he wouldn't have to eat on his own.'

'I don't think so.'

'Why not? Doesn't he like us?'

'He likes us fine. Get into your pyjamas before Nana and Grandad arrive.'

Her mother had raised her eyebrows when Beatrice told her the reason she was asking her to babysit. 'Is there something going on I should know about?' Deborah had asked.

'Definitely not,' Beatrice had replied, then went on to explain why she was going out to dinner with him, and that it was purely platonic.

Her mum hadn't been entirely convinced. But why should she be, when Beatrice wasn't entirely convinced herself? Her feelings for Mark Stafford hadn't been platonic back then, and they weren't platonic now.

She put the finishing touches to her make-up and sat back to check her appearance. She couldn't do anything about the fine lines around her eyes (whatever claims they made, no creams were able to reverse the effects of aging) but she looked okay. She'd done her best, and she just had to accept that she wasn't twenty anymore. Or even thirty. She'd be happy with thirty. Thirty wasn't even halfway. Forty, on the other hand, could very well be.

She'd already laid out her dress, and she shimmied into it, contorting herself into odd shapes as she struggled to do up the zip. With the addition of a clutch bag and a pair of heels, she was ready.

Hearing her parents let themselves in and Sadie's excited voice, she hurried downstairs, hanging onto the handrail, worried she might fall. Maybe she should change into her boots? The heel wasn't as high, but they didn't really go with the dress.

'Hello, darling, you look nice,' Deborah said, scanning her from head to toe.

'I said that!' Sadie cried.

'Thanks, Mum.' Beatrice turned to Sadie. 'Where's your sister?'

'Here.' Taya was slouching against the living room wall. She didn't look happy. Beatrice wanted to ask her what was wrong, but she didn't have time because the doorbell rang.

Mark was here.

Her heart leapt, missed a beat, then thudded as it caught up with itself, catching her by surprise and she coughed to cover it.

Lifting her coat off the hook in the hall, she hurried to open the door. Sadie was right behind her, and the child managed to squirm through it before it was fully open.

'Would you like to see my toadstool costume?' she cried, launching herself at Mark.

Mark gave her a hug, his eyes meeting Beatrice's. She shook her head. 'Your mum and I will be late if we don't get a move on. Another time,' he said.

'Promise?'

'I promise.'

'Anyway,' Deborah piped up, 'it's not finished yet, young lady.' She was gazing curiously at Mark.

Beatrice sighed. 'Mark, you remember my mum and dad?' Her dad was hovering in the background.

'I do. Nice to see you again.'

Deborah said, 'You too, Mark. How are your parents? Well, I hope?'

Beatrice stepped in, saying, 'We've got to go,' and she ushered him away from the door. 'Bye, girls. Bye Mum, Dad. I won't be late.' She pulled the door shut behind her and blew out her cheeks, wishing she had arranged to meet him at the restaurant.

They fell into step, their breath clouding in the cold air, and Beatrice hunted around for something to say. 'How did the art class go?'

He glanced at her. 'You heard?'

'It's all over the village.'

'Oh, god. Nothing bad, I hope?'

'The class loved it, but did **you?**'

'I did, actually. I've never really thought about the process before – not consciously – so I think I learnt something too.'

'Melanie is a hoot, isn't she? She's been singing your praises.'

'She's lovely.' He glanced at her again. 'So are you. I mean, you look lovely. Very nice.'

Beatrice spluttered and began to laugh. 'Very **nice?**'

'Beautiful. You look beautiful.'

'Okay, there's no need to overdo it.'

'I mean it. You do. You always did.'

What the hell was she supposed to say to that? She blushed furiously, and it made her cross. He wasn't supposed to compliment her: this wasn't how this evening was supposed to work.

They walked along the high street in silence, Beatrice feeling embarrassed. Mark didn't appear at all bothered. She concentrated on the festive displays in the windows and the lights twinkling overhead, and told herself that he was just being friendly. She also told herself that even if he wasn't, he would be gone before Christmas, his time in Picklewick fleeting.

Then she told herself for the second time that he was just being friendly.

Arriving at the restaurant, Mark held the door open for her. 'After you.'

She smiled politely and stepped inside, the warmth making her cheeks glow.

Otto came forward to greet them. He was wearing chef's whites, and Beatrice hoped their arrival hadn't taken him away from his kitchen duties.

'If you're out here, who is in there?' she asked, after he'd shown them to a table.

'Actually, I was hoping Mark could give us a hand,' Otto replied with a chuckle. 'The Wild Side appears to be the only place that hasn't nabbed him for one thing or another. I bet you never thought you'd end up being a Grinch?'

Mark shook his head. 'No, I didn't, and I can't believe I did it **twice**. Please don't tell me Dulcie is short-handed again?' he pleaded.

'Relax, you're safe. Let's get your drinks sorted and I'll send your server over with the menu. Enjoy your meal.'

'Thanks, I'm sure we will,' Beatrice said. She opened the menu and kept her eyes firmly on it. Everything sounded delicious, but she was having difficulty focusing. Her mind was stubbornly on the man sitting opposite. Did he really think she was beautiful, or had he just been saying that?

When their server arrived to take their order, Beatrice picked the first thing her eyes landed on. She was sure it would be delicious. Whatever it was.

With the menus whisked away and the starters yet to arrive, Beatrice was once again left with no idea what to say.

Luckily, Mark did — although after a while she began to wish he'd kept his mouth shut.

It began innocently enough. 'Being back in Picklewick, is like I've never left. I can't believe where all those years have gone,' he said.

'Me, neither. They've flown by.'

'Whenever I thought about the people I knew, Lisa, **you…**' He lingered on the word. 'I always thought of you as the way you were back then.'

'Sorry to disappoint,' she quipped, her heart fluttering.

'You don't disappoint. You never did.'

'You dumped me!' Oh, hell. Why was she bringing this up? What an idiotic thing to say.

'I did.' His voice was gentle. Regretful? Surely not. 'I hurt you,' he added, gazing at her intently.

Beatrice looked down and fiddled with the stem of her glass. 'Nah, it was fine. **I** was fine. I think. I can't really remember.'

'I think you can.'

'No, honestly, I can't. **Obviously** I remember you dumping me, but I don't remember how I felt.'

'Yeah, you do.'

'Are you on some kind of ego trip? Like, do you think that you're the one who got away, and I've been pining for you ever since? I'll have you know I've got two kids. They have a father. I slept with him. Twice. More than twice. A lot. So I haven't been pining for you.' She became aware that the gentle hum of conversation in the room had dimmed considerably. Oh god, had everyone heard?

'He was an arse,' Mark reminded her.

'I loved him.'

'But he turned into an arse. You said so yourself.'

'So were you.'

'I was not!' Mark looked affronted. 'Just because I ended our relationship doesn't mean I was an arse.'

Beatrice gritted her teeth. 'What are you playing at, Mark?'

'I'm not playing at anything.'

'Okay, I'll try again. Why are we here? You could have eaten here on your own – or not dined here at all. Dulcie wouldn't have minded. Why were you so insistent that I accompany you?'

'I wanted to talk to you, on your own.'

'What about?'

He huffed, and ran his hand through his hair, muttering, 'I don't know anymore.'

'I'll ask again; what are you playing at?'

'Bea, I—' He pulled a face. 'I don't know how it happened, but you've got under my skin.'

'Is that right?' Pull the other one, she wanted to add, but was interrupted by her starter being placed in front of her.

'Parmesan?' the server offered.

'Not for me, thanks.'

'Sir?'

'No. Thank you.' He stared at his food but made no move to eat it, his fork lying untouched. When the server moved away, he said, 'We were very young. Barely more than kids.'

'So?'

He shrugged, lifting one shoulder. 'We weren't ready for anything heavy.'

'**You** weren't.'

'No...' He chewed on his lip. 'I did care for you, Bea. More than you realised.'

'You had a strange way of showing it.'

'I didn't think you were into me as much as I was into you.'

Beatrice snorted. 'We spent ten months in each other's pockets. We were bloody inseparable. I'm surprised you didn't enlist the help of a surgeon to cut us apart. How could you not think I wasn't,' she quoted with her fingers, '**into you?**'

'And three weeks.'

'Excuse me?'

'Ten months and three weeks.'

That took the wind out of her sails. 'How—?' she began. 'You kept **count?**'

He shrugged again, looking away.

Could she have got it wrong? Had he ended the relationship because he'd thought she didn't care? Confusion pulsed through her, beating in time with her heart, rushing along her veins.

However, she refused to let it show.

'Why are we even discussing this?' she persisted. What was the point? The past was done and dusted. Whatever they once had, or might have had, was over. Long gone.

'Because since I've been back in Picklewick, I can't get you out of my mind.'

'But you... This can't... 'she stammered, then tried again. 'You're leaving soon.' She squeezed her eyes shut, opening them slowly.

'I can stay for as long as I want. As long as **you** want.'

Incredulous, she said, 'You're serious.'

'Do you ever wonder what would have happened if we'd stayed together?'

'Yes,' she breathed.

'Is everything alright with your meals?'

Beatrice jumped. 'Um, yes, fine, thanks.'
She had yet to taste a single morsel.

Mark waited until the server was out of
earshot. 'Shall we start afresh, see where
it takes us? No promises, no
recriminations.'

'I knew it,' she muttered.

'Knew what?'

'That this was a date. I thought you said
it wasn't?'

'Do you want it to be?'

'Do **you?**' she countered.

'I do. Very much. Can I kiss you at the end of it?'

'Don't push your luck, buster,' Beatrice growled, but inside she was singing. This could be the start of something wonderful – for the second time.

Beatrice clung to Mark's arm, giggling as she tried to get the words out. Walking whilst laughing fit to burst wasn't easy, especially in these heels, even with him propping her up.

'What about that time...?' she began, then doubled over, tears running down her face.

Mark was laughing too, but she had a feeling he was laughing because **she** was. 'What time?' he asked.

'You know, when you— Oh god, I'm going to wet myself.'

'Please don't. You'll ruin your shoes.'

Beatrice crossed her legs, wheezing as she tried to breathe through her laughter. 'Stop, you've got to stop. I can't take any more.'

She blamed her state of silliness on the wine. Since having the kids she'd become a lightweight. Two glasses and she was anyone's.

They had begun reminiscing during the main course, and by the time they'd finished their coffees and were heading out of the door, they'd been laughing hysterically. It was a wonder Otto hadn't thrown them out: trust her to bring down the tone of the place.

And now she looked like a drunk who needed help to get home. Thankfully there weren't too many people strolling along Picklewick's high street this evening to witness her debauchery.

Gradually she regained control and straightened up, uncrossing her legs. The control was fragile though, and she was likely to lose it at any moment. She could feel the giggles bubbling away beneath the surface, waiting for a chink in her armour to explode into hysterical life again.

'I must look a mess,' she said, dabbing at the skin underneath her eyes with the pad of her ring finger. The mascara was probably all down her face by now, and she bet her nose was red.

'We used to have fun, didn't we?' Mark said softly.

'We did....'

'We still could.'

Her eyes flew to his face. He wasn't joking. His expression was serious.

He said, 'I meant it when I said we could start again.'

'I know.' She didn't. Not for certain. But she wanted to believe him.

He held her gaze. The atmosphere had abruptly changed. It was charged, electric, like the air before a storm. She couldn't breathe. He was close, coming closer, his eyes filling her vision, his breath warm on her face.

And then he kissed her.

CHAPTER SEVEN

Beatrice's eyes flew open. One second she'd been fast asleep, the next she was totally and utterly awake. **What had she done?**

'It was a kiss, just a kiss,' she muttered, but the dream she'd just woken from had been so much more.

Oh, boy...

Hot and flustered, she pushed the covers back and got out of bed, the soft darkness hiding her flaming cheeks. A cold shower might be in order before she woke the girls.

Padding quietly into the bathroom, she pulled the light cord and winced as she caught sight of herself in the mirror. From the glow on her face and the sparkle in her eyes, she looked like she'd done far more than kiss Mark. And in her dreams, she **had**.

She hoped she hadn't looked like this when she'd got in last night, because if so, her mother would be asking questions. Ones that Beatrice didn't have any answers to.

Despite her intention to have a cold shower, Beatrice wimped out and turned the dial up. It was bloody freezing in here: the temperature had dropped overnight and she'd forgotten to set the heating to come on, and as she waited for the water to warm up, she asked herself again, what had she done?

Filled with equal measures of dismay and excitement, she couldn't decide whether she'd been incredibly stupid or incredibly adventurous.

Maybe Lisa could enlighten her?

Shivering, Beatrice hurried to the bedroom to fetch her phone, the steamy warmth of the bathroom a welcome reprieve from the chill when she returned.

'Are you up?' she asked, when Lisa's sleepy voice answered.

'What time is it?'

'Hang on, I'm putting you on speaker.'

'What's that noise?'

She stepped into the shower, the hot water cascading over her head, the thought of a cold one long gone. 'I'm in the shower. It's six-thirty-five.'

'Why are you phoning me at half past six in the morn—? **Mark!** Did something happen?'

'I woke you, didn't I?'

'Yes, but I have to be up in ten minutes anyway, to get the kids ready for school. Go back to sleep Robin, it's only Bea,' she said to her husband, then to Beatrice, 'What happened last night?'

'Mark kissed me.'

'Bloody hell, Bea!'

'I **know**.' She lathered her hair, her eyes tight shut. 'He said I've got under his skin, and he wants us to start again.'

'Do you believe him? I don't want to rain on your parade, but he hurt you badly once before.'

'I think I do.'

'What are you going to do?'

'Give it another go.' She rinsed the suds out of her hair and reached for the conditioner. 'If I don't, I'll always wonder **what if**.'

'Just be careful.'

'I'll try. But Lisa?'

'Yeah?'

'I think it's too late for that.'

'That's what worries me,' Lisa said, before hanging up.

It worried Beatrice, too.

'You look like something the cat's dragged in,' Dave told Mark as he put a plate of bacon and scrambled eggs down in front of him.

'Thanks! That makes me feel a whole lot better.'

'Didn't you sleep well?'

'I didn't sleep at all.'

'Nothing wrong, I hope?'

'Not at all.'

'Is your room too cold? The temperature's dropped and there's an Arctic blast on the way. They reckon we're in for some snow. It's too early for snow, if you ask me. We don't usually get any this side of Christmas.'

'No, we don't,' Mark agreed.

Dave harrumphed. 'I keep forgetting you're from around here originally. Anyway, is your room warm enough?'

'It's fine, thanks.'

'You don't need a blanket?'

'No, honestly, I'm fine.' Mark realised that Dave wasn't going to leave him alone to enjoy his breakfast until he'd explained why he hadn't slept. 'I was working,' he said.

'All night?'

'It happens like that sometimes.' He'd been on a roll, finalising the drafts for the illustrations ready to send to his agent, and he'd also completed the cover art. After breakfast he intended to email everything off to Angela, and then he was going to have a well-earned nap.

Satisfied with Mark's reason for his sleepless night, Dave sloped off, leaving him free to reflect on the real reason he hadn't been able to sleep.

Beatrice.

My god, that kiss! It had blown him away. Had her kisses been as wonderful all those years ago? He had a feeling they may have been, but he'd simply been too much of an idiot to realise it at the time. His lips still tingled, he could still taste her, smell her...

Every time he thought about her, it knocked the breath right out of him, and his heart stuttered before finding its rhythm again.

He felt more alive than he'd ever felt, every colour brighter, every sound more vivid. It was as though he'd been in a fog all these years but it had now cleared. And if he felt like this after just one kiss…?

Leaving the bacon and eggs to grow cold on the plate, he pushed his chair away from the table. Can't sleep, can't eat – he was a walking cliché.

Take it slow, he told himself as he climbed the stairs to his room. He and Beatrice needed time to get to know one another again, because neither were the same people they had been half a lifetime ago.

But, by god, was he looking forward to it!

The shrill ringing of his phone woke him, and Mark reached for it, blinking owlishly. 'Yeah?' he muttered, rubbing his free hand over his face.

'Is that any way to greet your favourite agent?'

He sat up, shuffling up the mattress so his back rested against the headboard. 'Angela.'

'You don't sound very happy. Is anything wrong?'

'What time is it?'

'You worked all night, didn't you?'

'Guilty as charged.'

'It's not good for you.'

'What are you – my mother?'

'I'm the woman who has just this second heard back from Estelle. She's thrilled with your new manuscript. So am I. The artwork for the cover is stunning. I defy any little boy or girl not to love it. Santa Paws,' she chuckled. 'She says there's talk at Pinkymoon of a cuddly toy franchise. They want a meeting.'

'For Santa Paws plushies?'

'Exactly! They've got to move fast, because of the design and the manufacturer's lead times. They want to do a special boxed edition: a book and cuddly toy. It'll make a fantastic Christmas present. Oh, and Estelle wants to have a chat about the possibility of more in the series.'

'More Santa Paws books?'

'No, the other characters. The market for Santa Paws is limited to Christmas, so can you change the focus? The main character could be—'

'Hang on,' Mark interrupted. 'You want me to change the whole story?'

'Not exactly. Just the focus. Take it off Santa Paws and put it on one of the other characters. Santa Paws works as a Christmas release, but if we run with the series idea, then—'

'Can I think about it?' For Pete's sake, it had taken him long enough to come up with **this** story, let alone change it now. 'How many books are they thinking of?'

'That's what we'll need to thrash out. I've gone ahead and set up a meeting for Friday. Does that sound good to you?'

Not really, he thought. 'So, to summarise, Pinkymoon Publishing loves my book but they want me to change the story and the main character?'

'In a nutshell.'

'And we're meeting with them on Friday?'

'That's right. I trust you can make it?'

'I'll be there.' There was more than a hint of resignation in his voice.

'Fabulous. I know it's short notice but you're only an hour and a half by train.'

'I'm not in Bristol.'

'Where are you?'

'A little place called Picklewick.'

'Picklewick... Picklewick...? Where have I heard that name before?'

'On my author bio. It's where I grew up.'

'I thought your parents lived in Bath?'

'They do.'

'So what are you doing in Picklewick?'

Falling in love, that's what he was doing. And he didn't know whether it was wonderful or terrifying.

Beatrice was making a casserole for tea. She'd ummed and ahhed over what to cook, wondering whether to stick to what she was good at (and what the kids would eat) or whether to pull out all the stops and make something fancy. She'd ended up deciding to play it down. This was Mark, a man who'd been known to eat baked beans out of a tin, and cold pizza left over from the evening before.

He might be a hot-shot children's author, but he was still the same bloke she once knew. She hoped. Anyway, he had two choices – like it or go hungry.

Beatrice was beginning to wish she hadn't given in to Sadie's insistence that she ask Mark to tea this evening, but at least if he saw first-hand the chaos that was her daily life, it would make him realise what he was letting himself in for, if he **was** serious about wanting them to start over. After this evening, he may well change his mind. It was one thing knowing that she and her children came as a job lot: it was quite another seeing it in action.

As Beatrice tidied up the kitchen, the most recent copy of The Picklewick Paper caught her eye. Her mum had brought it with her when she'd babysat on Tuesday and had forgotten to take it home. Or had she left it on purpose, because it had a piece about Mark in it?

Beatrice had read the article twice, and the part she kept going back to was the bit where Mark had said he would be going home after Picklewick. She knew his home was in Bristol, but what she didn't know was how long he intended to stay in Picklewick. And when he did leave – which he must – what would that mean for any future they might have?

Right now, Beatrice wasn't sure of anything, despite what Mark had said, despite the way he'd kissed her. She supposed she would just have to take it slow, and try not to get in too deep, too soon.

When the doorbell rang, even though she was expecting it, she jumped. 'Can you get that, please, Taya?'

'I'll go!' Sadie yelled, charging to the door before her sister could respond.

'Mark!' Beatrice heard Sadie squeal, then she heard him say something in return, but she couldn't make out the words.

When he entered the kitchen, he had a small child hanging onto him for dear life.

'Sadie, leave Mark alone, he doesn't need you clambering all over him. Taya, can you lay the table, please?'

'Why do I have to do it?'

'Taya…' The hint of warning in Beatrice's voice was enough to persuade her daughter to do as she was asked, but wasn't enough to wipe the sulky look off her face. Honestly, Taya was getting more teenagerish by the day. Goodness knows what she would be like when she actually **was** one. Beatrice dreaded to think.

Taya didn't perk up much throughout the meal, but Sadie was lively enough for them both. She didn't stop talking.

Right now, she was in the middle of telling Mark all about the toadstool costume that her nana was making for her. 'It's got sequins, and glittery thread, and it sparkles. I like sparkles.'

Beatrice laughed. 'I never would have guessed. This child should be called Princess Sparkle.'

Sadie ignored her. 'It'll be the bestest costume and I'll be the bestest toadstool. Even better than the fairies because I can do magic, can't I Mark? You said so.'

'Real toadstools can, but you aren't a real toadstool. You're a little girl.'

'I want to be a fairy.'

'I want to be an astronaut and fly into space.'

'In a spaceship?'

Mark nodded.

'Fairies can fly. Can you come watch the play? Mummy, can he?'

Beatrice saw Mark's eyes widen and she decided to rescue him. 'I expect Mark will be busy, so he won't be able to come.'

Taya finally spoke. 'Will Dad be there?'

'I don't know, sweetie. I'll ask him.'

'He never comes to anything,' she grumbled.

Taya was right, Eric rarely went to any school events. Sometimes she wished he would put his children first for once.

Beatrice decided to change the subject, steering the conversation into less fraught waters. 'Are you doing anything special for Christmas?' she asked Mark.

'I'm going to my parents in Bath,' he replied, 'but I'll be back in the New Year.' He sent her a look that made her shiver with anticipation.

Then she sobered. He might be coming back to Picklewick, but for how long? His home was in Bristol, after all.

After tea, whilst he helped her clean up, he told her about his trip to London tomorrow, and she listened with growing dismay.

'It sounds very glamorous,' she said. Picklewick was a far cry from meetings with agents and editors, book deals and cuddly toy franchises. Would he want to come back?

'Believe me, it isn't. Most of the time, I'm cooped up in my house, trying to get the images in my head onto paper. It can get rather lonely. I envy you.'

'You wouldn't say that if you had to deal with this pair day in, day out,' she replied, the sound of squabbling reaching her. The children were arguing over what to watch on TV.

'I love this, being here with you and the girls,' he said, and her heart fluttered.

He stepped closer and his gaze locked onto hers. The air grew thick as he reached out to brush his thumb against her cheek, his touch electric. 'I want to kiss you.'

Her breath hitched and a rush of warmth spread through her, but she was brought back to earth by a shriek. 'I'm sorry, I can't. I don't want them to see... There hasn't been anyone since their father.'

He drew back. 'You've nothing to be sorry for – it's me who should apologise. I wasn't thinking. I just wanted to... The children come first, I get that. But please can you stop being so damned sexy?' he whispered.

He looked deep into her eyes and for a moment the rest of the world faded as she saw his hunger. It sparked an answering longing in her.

But was desire enough to keep him here? Was **she** enough?

She hadn't been the last time...

Mark parked the car on the drive, his eyes scanning the house. It looked drab and unwelcoming compared to the other houses in the street. All of them, except his, were readily embracing the festive season. It was a shame to let the side down and be the only Grinch in the street, but it was pointless putting any decorations up when he would only be here long enough to do some much-needed laundry and repack his case.

His meeting was at one p.m. – a working lunch, which suited him fine, because it meant he didn't have to take time out of the day to eat. He'd only left Picklewick a couple of hours ago and he was already missing it. Or should he say, he was missing **Beatrice**.

After a check around the house to make sure everything was in order, he had a shower, opened the post, then flopped down on the sofa with a sigh of relief. It was great to be back in his own place, with a proper sitting room and a kitchen. Living in one room, as nice as The Black Horse was, had become somewhat claustrophobic. The space of a proper house around him felt totally luxurious and the thought of going back to the pub and his one-room existence didn't fill him with joy. But if he wanted to be in Picklewick what choice—

Mark slapped a palm to his forehead. He was an idiot. A moron, an utter numpty. **Of course** he had a choice. He could rent somewhere: a house, a flat or a caravan even, although a caravan would have to have bloody good heating to see him through the winter, because it was freezing out there.

Fired up with enthusiasm, Mark drove to the station at Temple Meads a short time later and spent the entire journey to London searching for properties to rent when he should have been concentrating on the impending meeting with his agent and publisher.

For Mark Stafford, successful children's author, his book didn't seem quite as important anymore.

Sadie and Taya dashed into the house as soon as Beatrice opened the door, in a flurry of discarded coats and flying hair, and from the smear of red sauce around her youngest daughter's mouth as she shot past, Beatrice guessed their father had taken them to McDonald's for their tea.

Trust him to fill them full of additives and leave her to deal with the fallout. It would be ages before they calmed down enough to go to bed. At least it was Friday, so she didn't have to worry about getting them up for school in the morning. She had to go to work, but Mum was coming here, rather than her having to bundle them out of the house and drive them to their grandparents.

A knock on the door caught her by surprise and she opened it again, assuming one of the kids must have left something in their father's car.

Eric's hands were empty. 'Have you got a minute?'

'What's wrong?' Beatrice glanced over her shoulder worriedly. The girls had seemed alright, and from the sound of them charging around upstairs and yelling like a pair of banshees, they appeared to be fine.

'Nothing's wrong,' Eric said, to her relief.

'Do you want to come in?'

His gaze flickered to the stairs. 'Can we do this outside? I don't want them to hear.'

Beatrice's spirits sank. *Don't tell me he's got his latest girlfriend pregnant,* she prayed, *because if he had, he could bloody well break the news to his existing children himself. She wasn't going to smooth the way for him. On second thoughts, maybe she* **should** *tell them herself, because he'd only make a pig's ear of it and upset them.*

Beatrice glowered and stepped outside, pulling the door shut behind her. Blimmin' heck it was cold! 'Well?' she demanded, crossing her arms and shivering.

Eric stuffed his hands into his coat pocket, and she almost growled in annoyance. He looked warm and cosy in a puffer jacket so thick that it could probably be worn up

Everest, whilst she was freezing her ears off waiting for her ex to announce that he was going to be a father again for the third time.

'It's Taya,' he began. 'She isn't happy.'

'Excuse me?' If he'd told Taya already, Beatrice just might make sure he'd be incapable of having any more children, ever.

'This new chap of yours,' he continued. 'The author bloke. Taya doesn't want you to see him.'

Beatrice blinked as she struggled to get her head around what he was saying. 'Why? What has she told you?'

'That you've got a boyfriend and lied to her about it.'

'I didn't lie!' Beatrice retorted hotly. 'He wasn't my boyfriend.'

Eric picked up on her use of the past tense. 'But he is now?'

She pursed her lips and glowered. She had no idea what Mark was. Anyway, what gave Eric the right to comment on *her* love life? He had a different woman every week and Beatrice never uttered a peep, unless it concerned the kids.

As though he'd read her mind, he said, 'I know it's not my place to say anything – who you go out with is your business – but Taya seems really upset.'

'Too damn right it's none of your business and Taya's only upset because, unlike **you**, this is the first relationship I've had since you left.'

'Since you kicked me out, you mean.'

'You deserved it.' She crossed her arms tighter, hugging herself in an attempt to keep the cold out and her temper in. 'I'm not going over this again.'

'Bea, I'm sorry.'

'Yeah, so you said – about a thousand times.'

'It was a mistake.'

Her brows shot up. 'Which time? The first or the second?'

'Both. I was stupid.'

'You can say that again! You stupidly thought you wouldn't get caught, and you were even more stupid to think I'd forgive you a second time. Eric, you're an arse.'

'I know. I was a shit husband. I admit I treated you badly, but I still care about you, I don't want to see you hurt.'

'That's rich, coming from you.'

'I read the article in The Picklewick Paper. He might be from around here originally, but he'll be gone soon and—' His eyes widened. 'Did you used to know him? You went out with him, didn't you?' His tone was accusing.

'What if I did? It was long before I met you.'

'He's turned your head, coming back here, flashing his cash. Taya told me he took you to dinner in that restaurant run by that London chef, whatshisname... Otto York.'

Beatrice blew out her cheeks, not bothering to explain.

'Look,' he said, 'it's Taya and Sadie I'm worried about. I don't want them getting to know him, then him buggering off to wherever he came from. It'll upset them. Sadie already thinks the sun shines out of his backside.'

Beatrice was done with the conversation. To have Eric quote her own words back at her after she had asked him not to introduce yet another fly-by-night girlfriend to her children was the last straw. 'I'll take your concerns on board when I make my decision that it's none of your damn business who I date,' she growled.

Realising she was about to lose her temper big time, she snapped her mouth shut and without another word she turned on her heel and marched back inside, slamming the door so hard it made the windows rattle.

Bloody Eric! Who does he think he is? she ranted silently. It was alright for him to have a love life, but the minute she showed any interest in a man, he was warning her off? And to think he had the cheek to use Taya as a way to get to her. Obviously Taya was going to find it hard to adjust to her mother having another man in her life: it was only to be expected. And obviously Beatrice would put her children's happiness first. Her relationship with Mark was in the very early stages, despite their history, so it wasn't as though she was moving him in next week. She was going to take it one day at a time, and if it didn't work out, it didn't work out.

But even as she was thinking it, Beatrice knew she was already in too deep, and that if their relationship ended for a second time, she would be heartbroken all over again.

Mark was bone weary when he walked into The Black Horse on Friday evening, his suitcase in his hand. He'd been on the go all day and he was knackered. But after he'd unpacked and collapsed onto the bed, his brain decided it was time to give him a slideshow of everything he'd done, said and seen today, and within a few minutes his mind was whirling and he was becoming increasingly restless.

A glass of water didn't help, and neither did a long hot shower: he was still too wired to relax.

Maybe a walk would do the trick?

Dressing warmly, he slipped out the side door. It was only ten-fifteen, so the pub was still open, but he wasn't in the mood to speak to anyone, and especially not to Dave.

Letting his feet take him where they wanted, Mark re-ran the meeting in his head, but he simply couldn't pin anything down long enough to examine it properly. Every time he tried, his thoughts veered to Beatrice.

Should he tell her that he was planning on renting somewhere nearby? Was it too soon to be thinking along those lines? Would she even want him to make that kind of a commitment yet? Was he jumping the gun, and getting ahead of himself? Questions, questions... He had so many and he wanted to ask them, but he was too worried he would frighten her.

On the way to London, he'd pinged some enquiries off to a couple of estate agents in Thornbury, figuring that there was no harm in starting the ball rolling, and with less than two weeks to Christmas nothing much would get done beforehand. He knew it would take time to find a suitable property, and then there would be the rental agreement to sort out, the references and the finances, so he would probably be living out of a suitcase for a while longer.

There was also the Christmas period itself to contend with. He had promised to spend the festive season at his parents' house in Bath, and he was looking forward to seeing them, but part of him wished he didn't have to go.

Mark stopped outside a shop, the window softly lit by a twinkling tree, and as he imagined himself living in the village he was filled with a warm glow.

When his feet took him into Lavender Lane (of course they did: it had been inevitable), he noticed there was a light on in Beatrice's living room, which meant she was still awake. Dare he?

Mark dared, but instead of ringing the doorbell, he tapped gently on the window and waited. After ten seconds – which felt like an hour – he tapped again. A little harder this time.

He was rewarded by the twitch of a curtain as it was pulled aside, and

Beatrice stared out. When their eyes met and she smiled, relief washed over him. He had been worried she might be cross.

And when she opened the door and gestured for him to go inside, he realised just how **not cross** she was when she stepped into his arms. Her lips parted, her chin tilted, and her eyes drifted shut as his mouth found hers. His hands were in her hair as he kissed her urgently, and she snaked her arms around his neck, pressing herself against him.

Mark groaned and she let out a sigh. His blood was aflame, desire scorching through his veins, heating him from the inside out. As the kiss deepened, his hands left her hair and skimmed down her back to grasp her bottom.

He wanted her so badly, so very, very badly, that when she drew back, breathing hard, her cheeks pink and her lips swollen, it took every ounce of self-control he could find to release her.

She glanced at the dark stairs behind. 'I can't,' she whispered, her voice husky.

'I know.'

'I want to. More than anything.'

'I think I should go, before we do something we regret.' He barely managed to get the words out.

The look in her eyes as she said, 'I wouldn't regret making love with you. Just not here, not now,' made his pulse roar.

How he managed to tear himself away he didn't know, and as he floated back to The Black Horse, there was one thing he was certain of – not having this woman in his life was unthinkable.

CHAPTER EIGHT

What do you do when you can't think of anything other than the woman you almost made love to last night?

Mark tried to write, but that didn't work and he ended up throwing down his pen in disgust. He tried to draw, but the stylus went the same way as the pen. Reading couldn't keep his mind off Beatrice for more than two sentences at a time, and the programme he tried to watch just became a background buzz to his daydreams of her.

She dominated his thoughts, and he couldn't think of anything else. His lips yearned to kiss her, his arms longed to hold her, his—

For pity's sake, if he carried on waxing lyrical like this, he should seriously consider writing romance. And if he carried on being unable to come up with a storyline for the character that Pinkymoon wanted him to write about, then he just might have to!

Packing it in for the day, he shoved his feet into his boots, his arms into his coat, and ventured outside. This was the last-but-one Saturday before Christmas, and Picklewick's main street was surprisingly busy. Mark assumed that Thornbury would hold greater appeal for shoppers than Picklewick, but apparently not, so he decided to have a proper look around the village. Despite having spent over three weeks here, he hadn't had a good mooch around, but if he was going to be living here, maybe he should. Besides, he wanted to see if he could find a gift or two for Beatrice and the girls. And not only them: he had his mum and dad to buy for, as well as his brother and family. And so far, he had been too preoccupied to buy anything other than the box of soaps when he was at the farm last Saturday.

Thinking of the farm made him think of Beatrice (to be fair, **everything** made him think of Beatrice) and he wondered what she was doing now. No doubt she would be busy serving customers, but was she thinking of him at all? In spite of the glaringly obvious physical attraction they had for each other, Mark wasn't sure how she felt about him. She might be in lust, but was she in **love**? Her best friend had told him that Beatrice used to be in love with him back then, and hinted that she still was, but did Lisa actually **know?**

Mark wished **he** did, but he wasn't prepared to risk damaging this fragile connection by asking Beatrice outright.

Picklewick had a decent selection of shops for its size and all the usual suspects: baker, butcher, chemist, greengrocer, florist, pet shop (could he get Sadie a hamster for Christmas? No, bad idea), but nothing caught his eye when it came to gift buying. It didn't help that he had no idea what to buy girls. His brother had boys, and even then Mark found his nephews difficult enough to find presents for. And as for Beatrice... Perfume seemed too impersonal, jewellery **too** personal. In fact, should he buy her anything at all? If he bought her a gift and she didn't get him one, would she be embarrassed? Feel awkward?

Bloody hell! Who knew Christmas could be so complicated? Maybe something small, just to show that he was thinking of her?

Eventually, after a trip to Thornbury, he settled on a safe option for everyone – books. You couldn't go wrong with books.

Why do radiators tick when they start to warm up, was Beatrice's first waking thought on Sunday morning, and this was because it was the heating coming on that woke her. The second was of Mark, which wasn't unusual considering she'd thought about him constantly since she'd discovered he was back.

But when she peeped out through the curtains to see what kind of a Sunday it was, she let out a gasp, and thoughts of Mark were driven from her mind.

Snow!

Oh, my goodness! And it was quite deep, too. Ten centimetres, she estimated, possibly deeper in places. It was only six-thirty a.m., but everywhere was white, the snow intensifying the light from the street lamps, and when she opened the window to feel the spiralling flakes on her warm skin, the world was still and hushed, holding its breath.

A feeling of peace stole over her as she gazed at the magical scene, then excitement started to build. The girls were going to love this! **She** was going to love this.

Beatrice threw on a dressing gown and hurried downstairs. A substantial breakfast was needed prior to going out to play, as well as warm, waterproof clothes. But first, a cup of coffee, which she would hopefully be able to drink in peace, before the whirlwind that was her youngest daughter got up.

It wasn't to be. No sooner had Beatrice raised a mug to her lips, than Sadie charged down the stairs, squealing so loudly that Beatrice feared most of Picklewick would hear.

'Snow, Mummy, snow!' Sadie thundered into the kitchen, her wellies in her hand. She skidded to a halt, dropped to the floor and began stuffing her left foot into the right Wellington boot.

Beatrice swooped in to intervene, grabbing the wellies. 'Oh no, you don't, young lady. Breakfast first. And did you honestly think I'd let you play in the snow in your pyjamas?'

Sadie pouted. 'I was going to put my coat on.'

Beatrice gave her The Look, and Sadie tried a different tack. 'I'm not hungry.'

'That's fine, but you're not going out to play on an empty stomach, so don't think you'll make it outside any sooner by not having breakfast.'

'Aww.' The pout turned into a scowl. 'I'm not hungry because I've got tummy ache.'

Beatrice narrowed her eyes. 'If you're not feeling well, maybe you should stay indoors until you feel better?'

'You're mean.'

Beatrice felt her daughter's forehead. It was cool to the touch, so she didn't think she had a temperature. 'Be honest,' she warned. 'Do you feel sick?'

Sadie leapt to her feet. 'I did, but I don't now. Can I have a biscuit for breakfast?'

Beatrice laughed. 'No, you most certainly cannot. I'm making porridge.'

'Yuck.'

'You **like** porridge.' Beatrice always made it with creamy milk and added a teaspoon of honey.

'Not today I don't.'

'Toast, then?'

Sadie shook her head, but before she could continue to plead for a biscuity breakfast, Taya bounced into the room, as excited as her sister at the sight of snow.

Sadie grumbled, '**She** said we have to have breakfast before we can go outside.'

Beatrice raised her eyebrows. '**She?**' Whilst she could appreciate that Sadie was excited, she didn't appreciate her daughter's disrespectful tone, or claiming to feel unwell in order to get her own way, especially when it came to trying to wriggle out of school.

However, there was only a week left, as school would break up for Christmas on Friday. This coming week would be an exciting one, what with the school play and all the other activities that the teachers had planned, so Beatrice would see what Sadie was like in January. But for now, she wanted to enjoy the day, and that meant having fun in the snow.

Beatrice was in the middle of a snowball fight and losing badly (two against one wasn't fair), when she heard her phone ringing.

Using it as an excuse not to be pummelled any more (Taya had a terrifyingly good aim), Beatrice retreated to the kitchen to see who was calling.

It was Lisa. 'Beatrice, lovely girl, how good are you with a shovel?'

Beatrice unwound her wet scarf from her neck with a grimace and glanced out of the window. The children were now heaping snow together to make a snowman. 'You can't be snowed in. It's not that deep.'

'Don't be silly, of course we aren't. But it's set to freeze tonight.'

'So?'

'If it does, and the paths aren't cleared, they'll be treacherous,'

'The gritters will be out. It'll be fine,' Beatrice said, as she noticed more fat flakes begin to fall.

'For the roads, yes, but I'm talking about the paths around the school. Do you remember the last time it snowed? The school was closed for two days because the paths were so treacherous. Nikki reckons the same thing could happen tomorrow. But if we clear them, the caretaker can put salt down so they won't freeze overnight. The school car park also needs to be cleared. Nikki's fine as she lives in the village and can walk to work, but none of the other teachers do.' Lisa lowered her voice and Beatrice guessed that one or more of her kids were in earshot. 'It's either that, or the kids stay home from school. I know which I'd prefer.'

'Give me half an hour. Mine are outside.' She winced as a blob of melting snow trickled down the back of her neck. 'I'll get them changed into dry clothes and meet you there.'

'Bring them round to mine. Robin can look after them.'

'Will do. See you in a bit.' Picking up her sodden scarf, Beatrice pulled a face. She'd better take a change of clothes for the girls, because no doubt they'd get wet again.

She was about to ask them to come inside, when she saw she had a message from Mark, and her tummy did a somersault.

Snow! Are you out in it?

Have been. Going 2 school 2 clear paths

Want any help?

Meet you there. 30 mins?

He responded with a happy smiley face and a snowman emoji.

Beatrice stared at her phone for a couple of seconds, her heart thudding, anticipation swooping through her as she remembered him turning up announced but oh-so welcome, late Friday evening. How she'd managed to stop before things went too far, she didn't know. Thinking about it made her feel weak and breathless. She would have given anything for an hour alone with him...

She hadn't seen him yesterday, and she felt giddy at the thought of seeing him now. As she got the children ready, she told herself she couldn't let her feelings show, not in front of so many people. And especially not in front of the other mums, who would be watching any and all interactions she had with him as intently as a flock of beady-eyed hawks.

Although it had been common knowledge at the time that Beatrice and Mark had been dating, only Lisa knew how Beatrice had felt about him, and Beatrice wanted to keep it that way. The problem was, Picklewick was small, and she didn't doubt that everyone in it knew that she and Mark had been out for a meal together – **twice**. She suspected that rumours were already rife, but she was determined she wasn't going to fan the gossipy flames any further today.

Bundling the children out of the door, Beatrice hurried them down the street. Her children loved going to Lisa's house and she knew they'd have a great time. They wouldn't miss her in the slightest, not with Lisa's kids to play with and a continual supply of snow to keep them entertained.

Flakes were still falling when she tried to kiss them goodbye at the front door, but both girls brushed her off, eager to get inside, and Beatrice sighed.

'Typical,' she grumbled. 'They don't want anything to do with me when there's something more exciting on offer.'

'Here.' Lisa handed her a shovel. 'Stop moaning. You'd complain if they were hanging onto your apron strings.'

'So I would,' she agreed, hoisting the shovel so it sat on her shoulder. 'Heigh-ho, heigh-ho, it's off to work we go,' she warbled.

'Blimey, you're in good spirits considering we're about to get backache and blisters. I'll be bloody annoyed if no one else turns up,' Lisa growled. 'If it's just me, you, Nikki and the caretaker, we're not going to get very far.'

Quietly, Beatrice said, 'And Mark.'

'What did you say? I didn't catch that.'

'And Mark.'

Lisa stopped dead. '**Mark** is going to be there?'

'Yes.'

Eyes wide, she muttered, 'I should have brought another shovel!'

'I hadn't thought of that.'

Lisa brightened. 'No problem. He can borrow mine. I'll supervise!' She resumed walking. 'I think you've got something to tell me.'

'I haven't.'

'Liar. Have you slept with him yet?'

'No!'

'You want to, though?'

'Duh!'

'Okay, stupid question. Obviously you do. But do you think it's a good idea?'

'Probably not.'

'But you're going to anyway?'

'Please don't judge me,' Beatrice begged.

'I'm not. I'm worried about you, that's all. But as you said, if you don't, you'll always be wondering.'

Beatrice's smile was crooked. 'I've seen him naked before, if you remember. I know what he looks like under his clothes.'

Lisa elbowed her. 'That's not what I meant, and you know it.'

It was Beatrice's turn to stop walking. 'I'm worried too. I still love him, Lisa. I never stopped.'

'I get that.' Lisa put an arm around her, gave her a hug, then propelled her onwards. 'I must admit, I would do the same in your shoes. Go get 'em, cowgirl!'

'Fat chance with the kids around.'

Lisa gave her a meaningful look. 'They're not around now, are they? They're at **my** house.'

'Are you suggesting that I...we...?'

'Why not?'

'It's eleven o'clock in the morning!'

'What's that got to do with it?'

'I can't just rock up to him with a shovel in my hand and say take me to bed right now.'

'I don't see why not, but if you insist on a build-up, do your bit at the school, then suggest he goes to yours for a spot of lunch. But instead of food, you could-—'

'I get the idea. There's no need to spell it out.'

Lisa said, 'Me and Robin will look after the kids for as long as you need. Take your time.' She smirked and added, 'Don't I have the best ideas?'

'You do! I could kiss you!'

As they entered the school gate, Lisa whistled. 'Save your kisses for Mark. He's going to need them. Look at him go.'

Beatrice looked, and her mouth dropped open.

Mark, snow shovel in hand, was effortlessly clearing the path to the main entrance, his movements controlled and precise. He was coatless, and she could see the flex and bunch of the muscles in his shoulders and arms.

So could everyone else.

A surprising number of parents had turned up, and Beatrice noticed several of the female contingent watching him out of the corners of their eyes.

Mark seemed oblivious, as he concentrated on his path-clearing efforts. Beatrice, in turn, concentrated on **him**, Lisa's offer at the forefront of her mind. Trying to take desire out of the equation (which wasn't easy when the object of that desire was right in front of her), Beatrice attempted to be objective, but all she could think about was the way he made her feel.

And she realised there wasn't a decision to make – because **she'd already made it**.

Mark tensed as Beatrice's fingers stroked his chest, trailing through the fine hairs in slow circles. They were in her bed and she was curled against him, one leg over his thigh, his arm around her, and he was happier than he could ever remember being. For the first time in his life, he felt complete, his body satiated, his mind still, his heart full. So very, very full.

He didn't want this moment to end, though he knew it must. The afternoon was slipping inexorably into evening, and she would soon need to fetch the children from Lisa's.

With her hand still on his chest, her fingers continuing to stroke his skin, she said, 'I forgot to ask how your meeting on Friday went.'

'Not great,' he confessed. 'They want to turn Santa Paws into a series.'

She hesitated, her fingers ceasing their movement. 'Isn't that a **good** thing?'

'I've got to rewrite it, with the focus on one of the other characters. Poor Santa Paws is to take a back seat. They want to make him into a cuddly toy though, so there is that. And my publisher is talking about even more library visits and personal appearances. Apparently "my brand is robust enough to take it". Anyone would think I'm JK Rowling or David Walliams,' he huffed.

'But that's good, isn't it?'

'All I want to do is write my stories. I don't want to do the bits that go with it. But the market for children's books is tough, and my agent and publisher don't want me to lose any momentum.'

'Is that likely to happen?'

'Maybe.' Right now, he didn't care if it did. All he could think about was Beatrice.

Her phone rang, making him jump, and she sat up. 'I'd better get going. The girls will wonder where I am.'

Mark's gaze travelled down her bare back, lingering at her waist, before settling on the curve of her hip. She was beautiful.

He watched her hunt for her phone, her hand delving into the pocket of the jeans lying discarded on the bedroom floor, and when she looked at the screen, her mouth tightened.

'Hi,' she said, answering the call.

Mark got dressed and tried not to listen, but it was impossible not to.

'Fine, thanks... Yeah, a fair bit... No, it's stopped now... Sorry they're not here, they're at Lisa's. I'll get them to phone you when they get home.' She jammed the phone between her shoulder and her ear as she stepped into her jeans.

Mark looked away and pulled his shirt over his head. Was his fleece up here or downstairs? He couldn't even remember taking it off.

Beatrice said, 'Thursday at two o'clock... You will? Sadie will be delighted!' She glanced over at Mark then turned away, lowering her voice. 'I'll let you tell her yourself. See you Thursday... Bye, Eric.' Tossing the phone onto the bed, she said, 'That was my ex.'

Mark bowed his head. 'I guessed as much.'

'He didn't know whether he'd be able to make it to Sadie's school play, but he can now.'

'That's good.'

'Yeah, it is.'

He said, 'I hope you don't mind, but Nicki invited me as a guest of honour.'

Beatrice's smile was wry. 'Is that the kind of thing you meant when you said your publisher wanted you to do stuff?'

Mark took her in his arms. 'Yes, but they'll be cheesed off when they find out I'm not doing this for the publicity.' He kissed Beatrice on the nose.

'Why **are** you going?'

'To see Sadie in her toadstool costume, of course!'

Beatrice lifted her chin, offering him her mouth and he kissed her with renewed passion. When she ended it, his disappointment was acute.

'When can I see you next?' he asked, knowing he sounded needy but he couldn't help himself.

She lowered her head and murmured, 'I don't know. Soon, I hope, but with the kids...' She trailed off.

'I understand. They come first.'

Her head came up and she gazed into his face. 'They do. They have to.'

He kissed her again, this time a tender meeting of the lips. He knew they did, and he was okay with that, that's how it should be. Mark would fit in with whatever Beatrice wanted, because now that he'd found her again he had no intention of letting her go, and if that meant waiting until she felt able to welcome him into her family, he would wait for as long as it took.

Beatrice studied her youngest child as she shuffled into the living room, and thought she looked simply adorable dressed in her pink sparkly toadstool costume. Beatrice's mum had done a brilliant job: much better than Beatrice could have done.

But Sadie looked worried. Her little face was flushed and her eyes were huge. 'I don't feel well, Mummy.'

Beatrice had a flash of concern. 'Is it your tummy?'

Sadie nodded.

'I thought you were looking forward to being the best toadstool in the world?' Maybe she had stage fright? After Sadie's initial reluctance on being told that she wouldn't be playing a fairy, she seemed to have come around to the idea of being a toadstool. But perhaps, with the play only a few hours away, she was becoming anxious?

Beatrice placed a hand on Sadie's forehead. She did feel rather hot, but then, it was probably quite warm in that costume. She'd only picked at her breakfast though, which hadn't bothered Beatrice at the time as Sadie and Taya had been in a heated discussion about Rudolf's nose, and Taya hadn't eaten much of hers either.

The kids were wound up like spinning tops already, and there were still six days to go until the big day. As far as Beatrice was concerned, Christmas couldn't come soon enough.

'Shall we get you out of this costume? You'll feel cooler with it off,' she suggested.

Sadie nodded, and Beatrice helped her take it off. 'Is that better?'

'Yes,' Sadie replied but she still sounded rather subdued.

'You don't have to take part in the play if you don't want to,' Beatrice told her. 'I'm sure Miss Barnes will understand if you don't feel up to it. Would you like me to have a word with her?'

'I **want** to be in the play.'

'But if you're not well…?'

'Please, Mummy, I want to.'

Beatrice checked her forehead again, but couldn't tell if Sadie was any cooler. 'I'm going to take your temperature,' she announced, getting to her feet.

'Nooo…' Sadie was starting to get fractious.

'If you've got a temperature, you can't go to school.'

'I haven't got a tempacher My tempacher is good.' Her chin wobbled. 'Please, Mummy, I want to go to school!'

Beatrice thought for a moment, then relented. 'Okay, but you've got to promise me you'll tell Miss Barnes if you don't feel well and I'll come get you.'

'I will.'

'Promise?'

'I promise. Thank you, Mummy. I love you.'

'I love you too, sweetie. Let's go brush your teeth and round up your sister.'

Beatrice would take the girls to school and when she handed over the toadstool costume to Sadie's teacher, she'd have a quick word with her. Beatrice's gut feeling was that Sadie probably **was** a bit off-colour today but not unwell enough to be kept off school, and that anxiety at being onstage wasn't helping. Even though Beatrice was looking forward to seeing Sadie in the school play this afternoon and she would feel immensely proud of her daughter, a part of her would be relieved when this was over.

Mark didn't relish being the guest of honour at Picklewick Primary's Christmas play, but he was quite looking forward to seeing Sadie in her costume. After persuading her to take part, he felt he had a vested interest; besides, it was kind of nice to feel part of the community he would soon be living in. He was quite excited to throw himself into village life, even if that involved helping to clear snowy paths.

As he sat next to the school's Chair of Governors in pride of place in the front row, Mark ran his thumb across the fading callouses on his palm, remembering the feel of the shovel in his hands. It had been a while since he'd done manual labour, but he hadn't minded it, not if it meant he'd got to spend time with Beatrice. Deciding it would be better not to dwell on what had happened afterwards (as wonderful as it had been, this was neither the time nor the place for thoughts like that) Mark focused his attention on his surroundings.

The hall was filling up with parents, grandparents and younger siblings –

those little ones who had yet to start school – and the noise was steadily building. He glanced around, hoping to catch a glimpse of Beatrice, but caught Lisa's eye instead. Giving him a wide smile, she pointed to her right and mouthed, 'Over there.'

Nodding to show he understood, Mark looked over his shoulder.

There she was, three rows back and looking so beautiful that she took his breath away. Beatrice was sitting next to her parents, but there was an empty seat beside her and when a man tapped her on the shoulder and sat down in it, Mark guessed that the bloke was Eric.

He stared at him, consumed by curiosity, but looked away when he saw that Beatrice had noticed. The last thing he wanted was to make her feel awkward or to draw attention to her. Or himself, for that matter.

The chatter subsided when a line of children was ushered into the hall accompanied by a teacher, filing in one by one to sit cross-legged on the floor in front of the stage. Taya was amongst them, and he smiled. Her lips twitched in response, broadening into a wide beaming smile when she spotted her parents. Ruefully, Mark realised he had a while to go yet before he won Taya over. She was understandably wary of him, and he could fully respect that. He hoped that in time she would come to accept him.

The headteacher called for silence, and when she was happy that the audience was paying attention, a small boy walked self-consciously onto the stage and read out an introduction in a faltering voice.

Mark settled back in his seat to enjoy the show. There was something incredibly sweet about the way the children threw themselves into their parts, despite clearly being nervous. The lead fairy was adorable, and he could see Sadie watching her, a frown on her little face. It seemed to him that she hadn't fully embraced being a toadstool and was still coveting the fairy role.

The toadstools had just shuffled into position in a semi-circle around the fairies, who were singing a song at full volume and mostly out of tune, when Sadie fell over.

Expecting her to get back on her feet, it took Mark a moment to realise she wasn't moving.

There was an abrupt silence as the headteacher hurried forward and bent down to check on her, then straightened up, her face ashen.

The next few minutes were a blur, and Mark could only watch helplessly as Beatrice leapt onto the stage to scoop her small daughter into her arms. The terrified expression on her face pierced his heart and he made to go to her, but Lisa grabbed hold of his arm and he realised Eric was there.

He heard someone say, 'Call an ambulance,' but Eric shook his head.

Taking Sadie from Beatrice, he said, 'It'll be quicker by car.'

Mark watched him carry his limp and lifeless daughter out of the hall, Beatrice by his side, shouting, 'Mum, look after Taya!'

Then she was gone. And all Mark could do was pray.

CHAPTER NINE

'You should go home and rest, I'll stay with her,' Eric whispered, and Beatrice opened her eyes to see her ex-husband standing by Sadie's bed.

Her gaze flew to her sleeping daughter, tiny and pale, a needle in the back of her little hand, and she gulped back fresh tears. 'I'm not going anywhere. I'm staying here.' She kept her voice low, so as not to disturb the other patients on the ward.

'You'll be no good to her if you make yourself ill.'

'You've been here all night too,' she pointed out.

He shrugged. 'I'm used to it.'

'She will be alright, won't she?'

'She will, I promise.'

The tears spilled over. She'd done so much crying over the past twelve hours, she felt wrung out, but they kept coming. 'I should have known,' she said. She'd uttered the same thing over and over since Sadie had been rushed into theatre yesterday.

'Don't beat yourself up over it. I'm a nurse and **I** didn't realise.'

'You aren't with them all day, every day. How **could** you realise?'

'How could **you?** The symptoms of appendicitis can easily be mistaken for so many other things, and it's rare in children as young as Sadie.'

'I should have realised,' she repeated stubbornly.

Sadie's eyelids fluttered and Beatrice leapt to her feet, bending over the bed. 'I'm here, darling, Mummy is here.'

Eric said, 'She'll sleep for a while and when she does wake up she'll be groggy. Go home and rest.'

'Nuh-uh.' Beatrice shook her head, sitting down again when Sadie showed no further signs of stirring. 'I'm going to be here when she wakes up. I'm not going anywhere.'

'At least let me get you something to eat. The staff canteen is open 24 hours.'

'I'd love a coffee.'

'You've had nothing to eat since lunch yesterday,' he argued.

'I've got enough padding to keep me going for a while. Missing a meal or two isn't going to kill me. What time is it?' She'd lost track after the lights on the children's ward had been dimmed for the night.

'Four-forty.'

Too early to phone Taya. No doubt she was exhausted after the awful events of yesterday, but Beatrice had spoken to her last night to tell her that her sister was okay after her operation and was now sleeping. She'd done her best to sound reassuring, keeping her tone bright and cheerful, and she hoped she had put Taya's mind at rest. It was also too early to phone her mum, even though she desperately wanted to hear her mother's voice. She could do with a hug too, but she'd have to wait until later – if Sadie was allowed visitors.

However, Beatrice wouldn't be speaking to **anyone** if she didn't charge her phone. 'You wouldn't happen to have a charger handy, would you?' she asked.

'I'll see if I can borrow one, and I'll get you a coffee at the same time. Are you sure you don't want anything to eat?'

'I'm sure.' As he turned to leave, she said, 'Eric? Thank you.'

'For what?'

'For being here.'

'She's **my** daughter too.' He hesitated. 'I'd never forgive myself if anything happened to either of them. Or to you. I still love you, Bea.'

He left her with those words ringing in her ears, but she was too weary to think about them right now.

Her only focus was her daughter, and how badly she'd let her down.

Mark's finger hesitated over Beatrice's phone number. He was desperate to call her, anxious for news, but he didn't know whether she'd welcome it.

He'd had a single message from her late last night. It had been brief.

Appendicitis. She's had an operation. It went ok x

He'd read it several times, each time hoping it might reveal new information. So far, it hadn't.

Oh, sod it. At least if he messaged her, she would know she was in his thoughts. He assumed she was still at the hospital and had probably spent the night there, so even though it was early he sent it anyway. If she did happen to be asleep, it would be waiting for her when she woke up.

How is Sadie?

It seemed rather abrupt, so he sent another. Anything I can do? x

Then he waited in vain for a reply, checking his phone obsessively.

He'd showered and had just sat down for breakfast when his phone rang. His relief was immense when he heard Beatrice's voice.

She said, 'She's awake and hungry, and asking when she can go home.'

'Thank god. How are you?'

'Tired, waiting to speak to the doctor.'

'Do you need anything?'

'No, thanks. Mum will see to it. She's coming in this afternoon and bringing Taya.'

'Is Taya okay? It must have been frightening for her. And for you.'

'She's fine; worried, but she'll be okay when she sees Sadie for herself. Hang on...' Her voice faded and he heard her say, 'No, it's Mark.' Returning to normal, she said, 'Sorry, that was Eric; he thought I was on the phone to Taya.'

The memory of Eric's face as he strode out of the school hall with his daughter in his arms, leapt into Mark's mind. The man had looked distraught, and Mark could only imagine what he'd been feeling. No matter how badly Eric had treated Beatrice, he loved his children.

'It must have been a terrible shock, for all of you,' Mark said.

'I blame myself.'

'**Why?**'

'I should have realised—'

Mark heard a man's voice, then Beatrice said, 'I don't care, Eric, I **should have**. She'd been complaining of—' She stopped. 'Sorry Mark, Eric keeps telling me that it's not my fault.'

Mark didn't know much about appendicitis and what he did know had been gleaned from searching the internet last night, but Eric was right. 'It **isn't** your fault,' he said.

A weary sigh floated down the phone and he realised that nothing anyone said would make any difference: Beatrice was going to blame herself, regardless.

'Are you sure I can't do anything?'

'I'm sure, but thanks anyway. I'd better go.'

'Let me know what the doctor says?' he asked. 'And give Sadie a kiss from me.'

'I will.'

It was only when the call ended and there was no danger of her hearing, that Mark whispered, 'I love you, Bea.'

One day soon, he intended to tell her.

Deborah said, 'Do you think they'll let her come home tomorrow?'

'I hope so.' Beatrice plucked a grape from the fruit basket and popped it in her mouth.

Sadie pulled a face. She wasn't keen on grapes. 'I'm bored,' she announced loudly.

'I know you are.' Beatrice gave her mum a helpless look.

She was trying her best to keep Sadie entertained, but the child was sick of being in hospital. And so was Beatrice. She was astonished how she could go from being so terrified for her child that she couldn't breathe, to utter boredom in the space of three days. After the consultant had done his rounds on Friday and declared himself satisfied with how the operation went and with Sadie's recovery from the anaesthetic, Beatrice had hoped Sadie would be allowed home that day. But it wasn't to be. She had been kept in over the weekend, and for Sadie, by Sunday afternoon the novelty of being in hospital had well and truly worn off. There was only so much book-reading and colouring that she was prepared to do. And she was also fed up with watching TV, especially since the channels available were somewhat limited.

God help me if they keep her in for another day, Beatrice thought, although she couldn't see any reason why they would. The tiny wound on Sadie's tummy was healing well, she had been taken off the drip on Friday, and all her vital signs were excellent. In fact, apart from some discomfort at the site of the operation, Sadie was almost back to normal, and Beatrice marvelled at the ability of young children to bounce back from something that would take an adult a couple of weeks to recover from.

Hopefully, Sadie would only have to spend one more night in hospital, and she would be discharged in the morning. Apart from a quick dash home for a shower and a change of clothes, Beatrice hadn't left the hospital either, so she was almost swooning at the thought of sleeping in her own bed. Trying to catch forty winks in a hospital chair had aged her ten years, she reckoned.

Taya would also be glad when everything was back to normal, although the upside was that she'd seen more of her father these past three days than she'd seen for a long time. Both girls had. Working in Thornton General meant that Eric could pop onto the ward and spend a few minutes with Sadie during his shift. And he also visited her both before and after he started work. The rest of the time, if it was at all practical, he spent with Taya. And Beatrice could see how her daughter was flourishing now that she had so much of her father's attention.

To Beatrice's surprise, Eric had stepped up to the mark, and to her even greater surprise, he seemed to be enjoying it.

There he was now, hovering at the entrance to the ward.

He was looking at her parents, and Beatrice guessed that he was reluctant to intrude on their time with Sadie. But knowing he was on his break and that he didn't have long, Beatrice beckoned him in.

'Mum, Dad, why don't you take Taya to the shop and buy her and Sadie a treat?' Beatrice delved into her bag for some money but her mum brushed her aside.

'I'll get it,' Deborah said. 'Come on Taya, let your dad have a chat with Sadie. You'll see him later.' She whispered to

Beatrice, 'He's taking her bowling this evening, but don't tell Sadie.'

'Gosh, no!' Beatrice agreed. Sadie would be furious if she knew they were going without her, and she made a mental note to suggest to Eric that he do something special with Sadie, just the two of them, when she was out of hospital.

Beatrice let Sadie and Eric have a few minutes alone, and she strolled over to the window. Yesterday had been the shortest day of the year, and today wasn't much longer. It would start to get dark soon, and Beatrice noticed that some of the nearby houses had already switched on their Christmas lights.

She frowned as she thought of everything she still had to do in preparation for Christmas Day. She'd not wrapped a single present yet, and she needed to do a big grocery shop. At least they were going to her parents for Christmas dinner, so she didn't have to worry about buying a turkey.

As she stood there contemplating Christmas, her thoughts drifted to Mark. She hadn't seen him since Sunday when they'd made love (the brief glimpse she'd had of him on Thursday during the play, didn't count) and she was missing him. He'd said he'd pop in to visit Sadie later, after her mum and dad had been, and she couldn't wait – though how she would stop herself kissing him, she didn't know. She hoped they could manage some time alone before he left Picklewick to go to his parents for Christmas, but with it being the twenty-second of December today, she wasn't sure whether they'd have the opportunity.

Sighing, she rested her forehead against the glass, then stifled a shriek when an arm crept around her waist.

Assuming it to be Mark, she squirmed around, only to be confronted by Eric.

Moving aside, she slipped out of his grasp. 'Don't,' she warned.

'Bea, listen to me, please. Seeing Sadie like this—' he gestured towards her bed and swallowed hard '— has been a wake-up call. I thought we were going to lose her.'

Beatrice gulped. So had she.

'It made me realise how much I've lost and how much more I **could** lose. I don't want to miss any more of their lives.'

'You don't have to. You can be as involved as you want.'

'You don't understand – I want to tuck them into bed at night and be there when they wake in the mornings.'

'You work shifts.' Her response was dry. If he thought he could guilt her, he could think again.

'You know what I mean.'

'Hmph.' She'd heard it all before. He'd sung a version of the same song when she'd told him she wanted a divorce.

She began to walk away, back to Sadie who was busily colouring something and was thankfully not taking any notice of her parents' exchange, but Eric grabbed hold of her hand.

Caught off-guard, she was pulled towards him and she came up against his chest. She put up her hands, but before she could push him away, he cupped her face and kissed her.

Beatrice froze. She was sorely tempted to knee him in the goolies for his audacity, but she didn't want to make a scene. Instead, she tensed, her eyes open, her lips unyielding, as she waited for him to get the message.

Realising he wasn't getting anywhere, he released her. 'Just think about it,' he pleaded. 'We were good together once.'

She opened her mouth to utter a scathing retort, when she realised he was looking over her shoulder, an unreadable expression on his face. And when she whirled around, she saw Taya standing by her sister's bedside, wearing a delighted smile.

Oh, sodding bloody fiddlesticks!

Mark staggered back from the doorway to the ward, the bag with the fairy outfit dangling forgotten from his nerveless fingers. **Beatrice and Eric were kissing.**

He felt sick and pain flared in his chest. He thought his heart was going to shatter with the force of it.

Taya glanced around and when he saw the happiness on her face, he wanted to cry. She looked ecstatic.

Mark wanted to stay and fight, to tell Beatrice he loved her, but he had to walk away. She had decided to make another go of it with Eric for the sake of her children, and he couldn't do anything to jeopardise that.

A middle-aged couple were walking towards him and Mark recognised Beatrice's parents and he turned away, not wanting them to see the anguish in his eyes. He had let Beatrice go once before, not understanding what he was throwing away. He would let her go again, but this time he knew all too well.

As he walked out of the hospital and out of Beatrice's life, he was sure he was doing the right thing, no matter how much pain it caused him.

At least Mark hadn't dumped her by text. Beatrice supposed she ought to be grateful for that small mercy. But a letter wasn't much better. Just more old-fashioned.

Lisa handed it back to her after she'd read it, and Beatrice threw it on the coffee table. She grabbed a cushion, hugging it to her chest and hitched in a breath.

'He didn't even use proper paper,' she said, as though the news of his departure would hurt less if it was written on a sheet of Basildon Bond paper, rather than a leaf torn out of a drawing pad. 'Damn him!'

She sniffled and Lisa passed her a tissue. '"Doesn't think it will work",' she quoted. '"It's for the best". Yeah, best for **him.**'

'More wine?'

'How many bottles did you bring?'

'Just the one.' Lisa topped up Beatrice's glass and she knocked half of it back. 'Steady on, you don't want to get drunk.'

'Yes, I do,' she replied grimly. 'But I won't. I can't, not with Sadie like she is. I'll save getting blotto for when she's fully recovered.' This was her daughter's first night home since she'd collapsed at school. The letter, such as it was, had been waiting on the mat when Beatrice had got home. Thanks Mark, she thought bitterly.

'You mightn't want to get drunk by then,' Lisa soothed.

'Believe me, I will.' Beatrice dabbed at her eyes. It had taken a herculean effort not to fall apart in front of the girls, but they were in bed now and if she couldn't fall apart in front of her oldest and bestest friend, then who could she fall apart in front of? 'I should have listened to you,' she said.

'You had to try.'

'No, I honestly didn't. I could have kept him at arm's length, but I just had to fall in love with him again, didn't I?' She sounded as bitter as she felt.

'You never **stopped** loving him,' Lisa reminded her. 'That was the problem.'

'I never should have trusted him. What is it with me and men? Do I have a sign saying "treat me like dirt" on my forehead? God, I can bloody pick them, can't I? First Eric, now Mark. He got what he came here for, an idea for his sodding book – which I gave him – and he had a bit of fun at the same time. It was a win-win situation for him, wasn't it?' She

350

drank the rest of her wine and held out her glass.

Lisa refilled it. 'That's your last,' she warned. 'You'll feel dreadful if Sadie wakes you in the night and you've got a hangover.'

'Stop being so bloody sensible!'

'No more wine.'

'It hurts, Lisa. It hurts so much. I thought we had something special.' She screwed up her face, the dam about to break. 'I guess the reality of a woman with two kids in tow was too much to handle.'

'He doesn't deserve you.'

'No, he doesn't. But that doesn't make it any easier. I wish he'd loved me back then. I wish he loved me now. But if wishes were horses, beggars would ride, and me and Eric would be back together. And we both know that's never going to happen.'

'You what?'

'It's a saying. It means— I don't know what it means. My nana used to say it.' Beatrice hugged the cushion closer.

'What about you and Eric?' Lisa was looking perplexed, and Beatrice realised she hadn't told her what had happened between her and Eric at the hospital.

'He wants us to get back together, to try again, for the sake of the girls. He says that Sadie's collapse was a wake-up call.'

'Are you going to?' She sounded aghast.

'No way. Eric and I are **not** getting back together. I did love him once, but he killed that when he was unfaithful. Taya's dearest wish is that we get back together, and to make it worse, she saw him kiss me.'

'Eric **kissed you?** When?'

'At the hospital. He caught me unawares. I didn't kiss him back, but Taya saw, and now she thinks there's a chance we'll get back together. I hate to disappoint her – it breaks my heart – but it's not going to happen. How can it, when my heart belongs to Mark?'

A creak sounded overhead, and Beatrice stiffened. Putting a finger to her lips, she shook her head, uncurled her legs and padded upstairs to check on the children, worried that Sadie had woken, but both girls were sound asleep.

Beatrice envied them. She had a feeling it would be a long time before **she** slept peacefully again.

The aroma of his mother's famous mulled wine permeated the house, filling Mark's nostrils with the scent of cloves and cinnamon. It was the epitome of Christmas, yet Mark couldn't remember a Christmas where he felt less festive. Today was Christmas Eve, but to him, it could have been any random Wednesday.

'I hope you're not going to mope around like a wet weekend, like you did yesterday,' his mother said. 'You've got a face that would turn milk sour.'

'I can't help the way my face looks.'

'Nonsense! Are you going to tell me what's wrong, or do I have to guess?'

'There's nothing wrong.' He dropped into a chair, wishing he'd gone to Bristol for Christmas. At least there he could be alone with his misery.

'Are you ill?'

'No, I'm fine.' Did being heartsick count as being ill?

'Are you having financial troubles? Because if you are, your father and I can help you out.'

'My finances are fine. But thank you anyway.'

'Problems with your book, your publisher, your Muse?'

'Not at all.'

'I didn't think so.'

'Why ask?'

'I wanted to be sure. What's her name?'

Mark tensed, then gave a small shake of his head and stared at the tinsel draped around the guilt-framed mirror above the fireplace.

'Have you fallen out, or is it unrequited love?' his mother persisted.

'You're not going to give up, are you?'

'I doubt it.' She opened her mouth to say something else but the shrill ring of the telephone in the hall interrupted her, and she bustled off to answer it.

Glad of the reprieve, Mark slumped back into the cushions and closed his eyes, the thought of trying to be jolly for the next few days filling him with dread.

His mother came back into the sitting room. 'It's for you.'

'What is?'

'The phone.'

'It can't be.'

'It is, if your name is Mark Stafford.' She gave him an arch look.

'Who is it?'

'Do I look like your secretary?' she demanded, then relented as he heaved himself out of his chair. 'She says she's your agent, Angela somebody-or-other. I didn't catch the surname.'

'Angela? Why is she calling me **here?**'

His mother tutted. 'Don't ask me – ask **her.**'

Mark sidled into the hall and picked up the handset. His parents had an old-fashioned phone with a curly cord. They called it retro; he called it archaic.

'Angela?'

'Thank god! I've been calling and messaging you for two days!'

'I switched my phone off.'

'Clearly. Is your computer off as well?'

'Pardon?'

'You're not answering your emails either.'

'It's Christmas Eve.'

'I sent it on Monday. And again yesterday.'

'How did you know I was here?'

'An educated guess.'

'How did you get this number?'

'Does it matter? Do me a favour and check your emails.'

'Why?'

'For god's sake Mark, just do it!'

'Wait there.' His phone was upstairs, so he went to fetch it, wondering what could possibly be so important, but not really caring. Surely whatever it was could wait until after Christmas.

He turned it on and went back downstairs while it caught up with itself, and when it did, he was assaulted by a barrage of notifications.

He said, 'Seven missed calls and nine messages? Really, Angela?'

'**Eight** messages.'

He looked again. She was right. She **had** only sent him eight.

The other was from Beatrice.

His heart clenched, a spasm of pain in the middle of his chest so acute that he gasped.

'I know, right?' Angela cried.

'What?'

'It's a tasty advance,' she continued and said something else, but Mark had stopped listening. He was trying to find the courage to read Beatrice's message.

Would there be any point? It would only make his heartbreak more acute. He'd suspected she might try to contact him, to apologise or to explain, and he hadn't wanted to hear it. He still didn't. Damn Angela for making him switch his phone back on.

'Mark? Are you there? **Mark!**'

'I'm here.' His reply was wooden.

'What do I tell Estelle?'

'About what?'

'The **advance**. Have you been on the eggnog already?'

'What do you suggest?' He didn't know what she was talking about and neither did he care: he simply wanted Angela to leave him alone so he could decide whether to read Beatrice's message or not.

He was leaning towards not.

'My advice would be to take it,' his agent said.

'Okay.'

'Great! I'll let her know and she can draw up the contract.'

'Fine.'

'You might sound a bit more enthusiastic.'

'Sorry... I'm thrilled. Honestly.'

'Good. A deal like that, isn't to be sniffed at. Right, that's me done. Have a lovely

Christmas and I'll speak to you in the New Year.'

'You, too.'

He replaced the phone on its cradle and stared at his mobile's screen. 'Let's get this over with,' he muttered, knowing that he would end up reading it sooner or later.

But when he opened it, it was the best Christmas present he could have wished for.

The living room was warm and cosy; the lights on the tree twinkled, and Christmas songs played in the background, Beatrice having insisted that the TV be turned off for an hour.

Taya and Sadie were in the kitchen making a gingerbread house, but making a mess would be a more accurate description, as there were blobs and smears of brightly coloured icing all over the kitchen table and all over the girls as well.

She was glad to see Taya having fun though, so she would put up with a bit of mess. Considering it was Christmas Eve, her eldest child was oddly subdued, and the only explanation that Beatrice could come up with was that the events of the past few days had affected her more than she'd thought, and now that things were kind of back to normal, it was beginning to catch up with her.

That was something else Beatrice blamed herself for, but she'd had to focus on Sadie – Sadie had needed her more than

Taya – but for a few days Beatrice had neglected her other child. And what really hurt, what she felt so incredibly guilty about, was the suspicion that she might have taken her eye off the ball when it came to her kids. She had been so wrapped up in her new job and her new (old) love affair, that she hadn't seen what was happening under her very nose.

No more. From now on, all of Beatrice's love, care and attention would be on her children. No distractions. And after Christmas she would have to have a serious think about whether she intended to carry on working. She loved her job, but if she hadn't been so worried about missing work and letting Dulcie down on Thursday, would she have listened to her instincts and kept Sadie home from school?

Rationally, she knew it wouldn't have made any difference – Sadie would still have needed her appendix removed. And by being in school and Eric being in the audience, Sadie had got to the hospital faster than if she had collapsed at home.

But all the rationalising and reasoning in the world couldn't prevent Beatrice from feeling as guilty as hell.

Lisa reckoned she was using the guilt to deflect from the misery of a broken heart, but Beatrice didn't think that was true, and even if it was, she'd take it, because anything was better than thinking about Mark.

The lights on the tree created a soft warm glow, but inside her, the chill of loneliness settled over her. She never should have let him into her heart again. The wound of his first abandonment had fleshed over, the scar on her heart still there, but buried deep. He had ripped it open again and it was now raw and bleeding, with a pain so acute she knew she would never risk loving anyone again.

Her heart ached, not just from his absence, but from the dreams she had woven in the quiet hours of her mind which were now lost. She had painted a future together in colours more vibrant than the pictures in his books. When she'd read his letter and understood that he didn't love her after all, her world had darkened, the colour leeched out of it. Hers was a story without a happy ending, and she hated herself for letting him write the first word on her heart.

Each day since he'd left had felt like a slow unravelling, a reminder of the love that had slipped through her fingers for a second time.

As she sat in the fading light, tears welled, but she refused to cry over him again. She'd shed enough tears, so with a shaky breath, she blinked them away and resolved to take it one day at a time. And if she never heard his name again, it would be too soon.

The doorbell rang.

With a deep sigh, she got to her feet. It was probably her parents. They'd taken to calling in most days to check on her and the girls. Sadie had scared them, too.

Sadie beat her to the door, thundering into the hall. 'Mummy! It's Mark!' she yelled.

Beatrice hurried after her. 'What have I told you about answering the door to strangers—' She stopped. It **was** Mark.

'Mark isn't a stranger,' Sadie said, grabbing his hand and trying to tug him inside.

Wasn't he? Beatrice had thought she knew him, but she hadn't. Not then, and certainly not now.

'Can I come in?' he asked.

'No.'

Confusion flitted across his face. 'I thought—'

'That you could rock up again and I'd welcome you with open arms?' She shook her head. 'I don't think so. Sadie, go to your room. You too, Taya,' she added, when she saw her in the kitchen doorway.

'Mum, let him in,' Taya said.

'Go to your room. Now!' She didn't want the children to witness this – whatever **this** was. Turning her attention back to Mark, she hissed, 'You'd better leave.'

'But you—'

'Go! Before I call the police.' She put her hands on her hips. She didn't know what game he was playing, but she wanted no part of it.

'Bea, don't do this to me,' he pleaded. 'You can't tell me you love me one minute, then tell me to go away the next.'

'I never said I love you.'

'You did!' He yanked his mobile out of his pocket. 'You sent me a message—' He stopped, the colour draining from his face. 'It wasn't meant for me, was it?'

'I don't know what you're talking about. I haven't sent any messages telling anyone I love them.'

He hung his head. 'Sorry, my mistake. I'll go.'

'Mum?'

'**Not now,** Taya. I thought I told you to go to your room.'

'**I** sent it.' Taya's voice was small. 'I borrowed your phone and sent it.'

'You did **what?**' Beatrice's gaze flew to Taya, appalled, and Taya began to cry. 'Why?' she demanded.

'Because I heard you talking to Aunty Lisa. When you got drunk.'

'I wasn't drunk,' she replied automatically. 'Taya, sweetie, what have

I told you about listening to other people's conversations? Especially adult ones, when you don't understand what they're saying.'

'You said you didn't love Dad, but you love Mark. Is it true?'

Beatrice groaned. 'I care for your dad, but—' Oh hell, how do you explain something that complicated to a nine-year-old.

'You and Dad aren't getting back together, are you.'

Her eyes filling with tears again, Beatrice said, 'No, Taya, we're not. But that doesn't mean Mark and I are.'

'Why not? Mummy, you're so sad now.'

Mummy? Taya hadn't called her that in a while. 'I'm not sad,' she fibbed.

'You are. You were really happy when Mark was here, and now you keep crying.'

Blast, she didn't think the kids had noticed. She'd thought she'd hidden it well. 'Please Taya, go to your room, and take Sadie with you. I need to have a quick chat with Mark.'

But Taya wasn't done with her yet. 'Mark saw you kissing Dad.'

Beatrice's mouth dropped open. She looked at Mark. 'Is that why...?'

'Yes.'

'You left because you thought...?'

'Yes.'

'**You eejit**.' She glared at her daughters and waited until they had beaten a hasty retreat up the stairs. 'Why didn't you ask me?'

'How could I? What could I say – Bea, I saw you snogging your kids' dad, but do you have any feelings for me?'

'That's exactly what you should have said.'

'I'm going to be honest – I love you, Bea. I think I always have, but I was too stupid to realise it. I don't want to lose you again. Can you forgive me?'

Beatrice didn't have to think about it. She had forgiven him the moment she realised that he was willing to put her children's happiness before his own. He'd walked away to give her and Eric a chance – because that was the right thing to do. Mark Stafford **was** a nice guy. How could she **not** forgive him?

To think Taya had sent Mark that message! It made her heart melt. Beatrice owed her daughter a massive debt of gratitude, and she was so full of love that she thought she might burst.

She said, 'I think you'd better come in. We've got a lot of catching up to do.'

Mark gathered her into his arms and kissed her gently. 'The catching up can wait. It's Christmas Eve. I'll call you later.'

'You're not going anywhere. You're going to spend it with us,' she replied firmly.

But before she called the girls downstairs, she wanted a minute to kiss him properly, and as their lips met, Beatrice's heart — like the Grinch's — grew three sizes.

Mark loved her.

Wishes did come true, after all.

Mark inhaled deeply and his mouth watered. The turkey smelt divine. It looked it too: white meat, crispy skin, and surrounded by golden Yorkshire puddings.

Beatrice's father placed the serving platter in the centre of the table with reverence, saying, 'My wife cooks a mean Christmas dinner. Mind you, by the day after Boxing Day I'll be sick to death of turkey.' He leant in and whispered loudly, 'If I'm desperate for a change, I'll pop into The Black Horse and have lunch with you – no doubt the girls will want to go to the sales, so we can have a sneaky pint and get to know one another properly.'

'I heard that,' Deborah said, winking at Mark. 'Little does he know, but he'll be looking after our grandchildren. I'll be damned if we're dragging Taya and Sadie around the shops. Help yourself, Mark. Don't stand on ceremony.'

Beatrice passed him a tureen of glazed carrots. The children were already spooning food onto their plates. Sadie, he noticed, was paying particular attention to the pigs in blankets, a determined expression on her face.

'They're her favourite,' Beatrice said. 'That's why Mum cooked so many, because she knew Sadie would eat the lot if I let her.'

'Thank you again for inviting me.'

'I was hardly going to let you starve.'

He chuckled. 'I'm sure Dave and Monica would have taken pity on me and made me up a plate.'

She squeezed his leg. 'And you would have ended up eating it on your own in your room. Not a chance.'

Mark had talked Dave into giving him his old room back, on the understanding that there wouldn't be any food served on Christmas Day – although normal service would be resumed on Boxing Day – so having not had any breakfast, apart from the complimentary biscuits in his room, Mark had been starving by the time he arrived at Beatrice's house shortly after noon this morning. They had agreed that he wouldn't arrive before then, so Eric could spend the morning with his daughters.

By the time Mark got to Beatrice's, he had found her sitting on the sofa with a Baileys Irish Cream in one hand, a Terry's Chocolate Orange in the other, and surrounded by toys and wrapping paper. The girls had been glassy eyed with excitement, their mother glassy eyed with exhaustion, having been woken several times in the early hours by Sadie asking whether Santa had been yet and worrying that the Grinch had stolen her Christmas, despite the green Grinch dust that had been sprinkled on the doorstep.

The children were happy to see him (probably because he came bearing gifts, and the books were enthusiastically received), and he had spent the next hour or so playing games with Sadie and showing Taya how to set up her new tablet, before accompanying them to

Beatrice's parents' house for Christmas lunch.

He had no idea what Beatrice had said to her mum and dad, but they had welcomed him with open arms, so Mark assumed it hadn't been anything too awful.

'So,' Deborah said to him, 'are you back in Picklewick for good?'

Mark shot an anxious glance at Beatrice. 'I hope so. If Beatrice is okay with that.'

Beatrice rolled her eyes. 'Why do men need things spelling out? I'm most definitely okay with that. But where are you going to live? You can't stay at The Black Horse indefinitely.'

'I don't intend to. I've already put feelers out with a couple of estate agents.' His original intention had been to rent somewhere, but if he sold his house in Bristol he could buy a place in Picklewick instead. And with the advance from Pinkymoon Publishers, he could afford to buy somewhere very nice indeed – somewhere with plenty of room for a wife and two little girls... When the time was right, he would ask Beatrice to marry him.

After a lovely Christmas Day spent with Beatrice's family, it was eventually time for the tired children to go home, and Mark walked Beatrice and the girls back.

He hadn't intended to come in. He'd intended to say good night on the doorstep, but Sadie had other plans and had grumpily insisted that Mark read her a bedtime story. He obliged by reading her favourite book, the one he had written and illustrated himself.

It had been the best Christmas ever, and when Beatrice took him to her bed much, much later; it was the perfect end to a perfect day.

And that was how Marc Stafford, renowned children's author, began the rest of his life with a woman he had loved for most of it, if only he had realised.

There are loads more large print books in the Muddypuddle Lane series. Available at all good book stores, or ask your local library.

About Etti

Etti Summers is the author of wonderfully romantic fiction with happy ever afters guaranteed.

She is also a wife, a mum, a pink gin enthusiast, a veggie grower and a keen reader.